What if the Sun...

(Si le soleil ne revenait pas)

What if the Sun...

(Si le soleil ne revenait pas)

By Charles Ferdinand Ramuz
Translated by Michelle Bailat-Jones
Foreword by Laura Spinney

ONESUCH PRESS

LONDON   MELBOURNE   NEW YORK

Onesuch Press enriches lives by reclaiming the forgotten past; publishing the lesser known works of great writers and the great works of forgotten ones. For more information visit *www.onesuchpress.com*

A ONESUCH BOOK

Published by ONESUCH PRESS

PO Box 303BK, Black Hill 3350 Australia

Si le soleil ne revenait pas
Short story first published in Lausanne, 1912
Novel first published in Lausanne, 1937
Translation © Michelle Bailat-Jones, 2016

© Onesuch Press, 2016

National Library of Australia Cataloguing-in-Publication entry
Author: Ramuz, C. F. (Charles Ferdinand), 1878 — 1947, author
Title: What if the Sun... / Si le soleil ne revenait pas
by Charles Ferdinand Ramuz
translated by Michelle Bailat-Jones
foreword by Laura Spinney

ISBN: 978-0-98-740147-2 *(paperback)*
ISBN: 978-0-98-740148-9 *(ebook)*

Subjects: French fiction.
Other Authors/Contributors:
Bailat-Jones, Michelle - translator
Spinney, Laura - foreword

Dewey Number: 843.912

The paper used in this publication meets the minimum requirements of ANSI/NISO Z39.48-1992 (R1997) (Permanence of Paper). The paper used in this book is from responsibly managed forests. Printed in the United States of America, the United Kingdom and Australia by Lightning Source, Inc.

Contents

Foreword

1937. War looms over Europe, and Charles Ferdinand Ramuz is only too attuned to it. "My life was a life of wars," he would write in his diary a few years later. So it was quite natural that he should translate that intimation of a slow and ineluctable slide toward hell into a fable about the approaching end of the world. And that he should set it, as he had so many stories, in the Swiss Alps—the Valaisan Alps, to be precise.

What might the end of the world look like, to people who inhabit high mountains, whose lives are governed by the dependable revolution of the seasons? Perhaps the sun might slip beneath a western ridge one evening, and not return in the morning. That was the primal fear that had been handed down through generations of *paysans*—countryfolk—and that Ramuz himself had inherited. Descended from a long line of winegrowers in the Swiss canton of Vaud, he carried it in his flesh and blood, in the sinews of the hand that held his pen. Being alive in the first half of the 20th century, however, he also knew that that terrifying prospect represented a mild version of hell. Real hell would be knowing in advance that it was going to happen. And so, revisiting a theme that he had explored many times before in his fiction—notably in a short story that he wrote in 1912, on the eve of another war—he bestowed upon the villagers of Upper Saint-Martin the dreadful knowledge that the sun was sick and would soon expire, leaving them to die alone in the cold and the dark.

The prophecy falls from the lips of the village sage and healer, Antoine Anzévui, whose words provoke a different response in each villager but leave no-one indifferent. The weather seems to bear him out. But the sun abandons those parts for a few months every year, so to accept the prophecy means to have faith in the prophet—to believe him when he says that the life-giving star won't return as expected in the spring.

The villagers soon polarise into two groups—those who believe Anzévui, and those who do not. Those who arrange their lives—what they believe is left of them—around his prediction, and those who carry on living in spite of it. These camps fall out roughly along the lines of age: the old accept, the young deny. But there are those who cross the lines. The young Augustin Antide turns to the wall rather than submit to the bedtime blandishments of his beautiful wife Isabelle, who emanates life, laughter and warmth. And when she happens to walk in on him and his parents, sitting morosely in the parental kitchen, "all three of them at once turned toward her, three destroyed faces, so much so that Augustin seemed almost as old as his parents".

What holds for Upper Saint-Martin holds for the rest of the world, because in Ramuz's novels the village is the world and the world is the village—even if the village is, in so many respects, cut off from that world, moulded by its very remoteness from it. So Arlettaz, bereft following the departure of the daughter he worshipped, welcomes the end because it means that he can stop searching for her at last. When Follonnier asks him if he still intends to go down to Le Bouveret, on Lake Geneva—the one place he hasn't looked—he replies in the negative. "Because we'll see each other again... because the sun, you know, it isn't just for us that it's going away, not just for us up here in Upper Saint-Martin, don't you know? But for everyone?"

The weather continues to deteriorate. Soon the sun can barely haul itself above that vertiginous landscape. Day and night mingle, and Ramuz captures the cloying, daylong dusk through which the villagers swim. The young Cyprien Métrailler leaves on his expedition to bring the sun back to the village, and during his ascent of the mountain steps out onto a ridge. Normally from that place you have a "magnificent view of the deserts of glaciers and rocks perched on high". But that morning he can only see a short distance in front of him, and turning round, a short distance behind. "A vague and limitless immensity of light fog, if it was truly fog and not a simple blocking of the daylight. Because the day has risen a little, although now it was no longer rising; it was immobile and somehow knotted up on itself."

The hold that Anzévui has over the villagers is not to be underestimated. When Cyprien finally finds the sun, it appears to him "exactly like a severed head around which the beard and hair still hung smoking". In his terror he runs helter skelter into a deep gorge, losing his gun on the way, and is only saved by the love of an elderly father. When that same elderly father lies on his death bed, it is Anzévui whom the villagers call. Sitting alone, watching the dying man, the old shaman speaks up. "Martin, I see what's happened; you just need to let yourself go." And the old man lets go. There follows one of the most sublime passages in the book, which in Michelle Bailat-Jones' translation retains all its poignant poetry, as the coffin of the blind Martin Métrailler is transported down to its final resting place in Lower Saint-Martin. The walls of shovelled snow that border the lane are now so high that the bearers must raise the black box aloft, causing it to rock back and forth "like a little boat on a little sea amidst the softness of the snow". "Was it to show you the countryside one last time, Métrailler, so vast and beautiful when seen from up here? Was it so that you could see it from above, as if you were soaring, as if you were in the air, like when the bird with his unfurled wings has all that great blue emptiness below him?"

Much has been written about Ramuz's experiments with viewpoint and the difficulties they pose for an English translator, who must choose which of one, you, we or they to substitute for the French *on*. In an earlier novel that Bailat-Jones translated, *Beauty on Earth* (1927), he used this ambiguity to explore the boundary between the individual and the collective in the presence of an existential threat from outside. There the threat was feminine beauty, here it is a dying sun, but the stories have this much in common: there is a point at which the individual and the group mind become interchangeable, at which the barriers between them come down, and it's that place that Ramuz is searching for—and finds—with his fluid and subtle use of language.

In January 1938, a particularly bright display of Northern Lights terrorised people across Europe, many of whom took it as a sign that the world was going to end. Episodes of collective panic, or mass hysteria, have been recorded throughout history, all over the world. But it's not because it has happened before and will happen again that you believe Ramuz's depiction of the village's transformation. It's because he remains true to the fundamental laws of the universe while deftly blurring the boundaries upon which we unthinkingly rely. He never asks us to embrace the supernatural, he only adds it to the natural, drop by imperceptible drop, as a painter adds water to colour.

The roads become impassable, the children are no longer allowed out, the blood drains from the adults' cheeks and they are obsessed by the urge to hoard. Faithful to fluidity, to ambiguity and hence to Ramuz, Bailat-Jones captures their slow weaving of themselves into a cocoon of fear. And just when you think that they will never emerge, that Upper Saint-Martin is lost to an endless winter, Isabelle—beacon of light, antidote to Anzévui's poison—steps out of the not-quite hardened chrysalis and lifts her face to the sun. The individual asserts herself and restores colour to the world, at least for a little while longer.

In the 1912 short story, which Ramuz gave the same title as this novel and which Bailat-Jones has translated here too, there is no such reprieve. Was the ageing Ramuz more optimistic in 1937, despite the accumulating portents? Was he raising a signpost to Europe's youth, or had he simply acquired the status of sage himself, and dared to make his own prophecy—the antithesis of Anzévui's, but one that also required its hearers to take a leap of faith? What if the sun... was his penultimate novel, published a decade before his death. He knew by then that his own source of inspiration would never dry up, that it would always be renewed. He knew, and wanted us to know, that in the Swiss mountains, as elsewhere on earth, winter follows spring and is followed in turn by another spring.

Laura Spinney
May 2016
Paris

Translator's Note

It can be fun to read a book that offers its central question right up front in the title. It feels so simple, so orderly—like the author just sat down one day and thought, I'd like to figure this one thing out, and then produced a solution. And it seems as if Ramuz did something along these lines. In 1912, while living in Paris, Ramuz witnessed a solar eclipse. He notes only the occurrence of the eclipse in his journal, but no reaction. Presumably, he was affected enough by the event to wonder about it, because over the next several months he worked on a short story entitled, *"Si le soleil ne revenait pas"* (literally, "If the sun were never to return"), which was published for the first time the following November in the *Gazette de Lausanne*.

It appears that this first story was not a full enough answer for him. Fifteen years later, Ramuz's Swiss publisher Mermod came out with a novel bearing the same title. It is a much longer answer to the same question, and it contains all that the intervening time period would bring to Ramuz's style and fictional project. In between the two stories lie the four horrible years of World War I, the planet's race to the atomic bomb and other preoccupying scientific questions and advances, as well as Europe's long escalation toward World War II. The novel *Si le soleil ne revenait pas* was written over two months in the spring and early summer of 1937, edited in August and published in November that same year.

But what does this idea of a question and its various answers mean for the task of translating the novel? On the surface, this is just one way among many of accessing the two related texts—how did Ramuz's response evolve across those intervening years? In the most fundamental way, there is an argument for very little difference: Ramuz sets up a fictional scenario in which nature presents an obstacle and civilization responds. Where it gets interesting for the translator is in how he sets up that scenario in terms of its narrative positioning and how this technique has shifted between the short story and the novel.

In the short story, Ramuz's first answer to the question of what would happen if the sun were never to return is quite straightforward. A mountain village awakens to complete blackness. No more sun. This is unequivocally the end of the world, an astronomical apocalypse. And in line with this straightforward idea, he provides a fixed and identifiable narrator who recounts first a group experience, and then a specific character's experience. This isn't to suggest the short story is in any way overly simple—it is very interesting in the way it fits into Ramuz's (and an entire generation of writers') overall concerns with apocalyptic themes, a recurrent focus throughout his entire oeuvre—but its complexity doesn't reside in any complicated point-of-view technique, nor does it pose any extraordinary translation challenges.

By 1937, however, his writing had developed a narrative ambiguity, a kind of layered narrative telescoping that would characterize all of his later work. This novel was written during the Spanish civil war, during a time of technological change and great insecurity, and its answer to Ramuz's question contains the kind of fragmentation that can be expected from a writer wholly attuned to modernism's preoccupations. Here the narrator is not fixed—is it an omniscient voice? is it a collective voice? The French language—with its impersonal *on* ("one", or "we", or people in general)—allows for this ambiguity in a way that is more difficult to render smoothly in English without sounding overly formal or informal. When Ramuz arrives at the start of a new scene, there is a moment when it feels like the narrator is experimenting with the right position. Perhaps the scene is best experienced from a single character, or perhaps from above, or no, perhaps from a group of specific villagers (the women, or the men, or the old people), or perhaps, finally, from a collective voice speaking for the entire village. There is a lot of slide and shift and his *on* can be hard to gauge, even more so when he punctuates his scenes with the other pronouns at his disposal, using *ils/elles/vous/nous* when he clearly wants or needs to be more specific. So this isn't just a question of an outdated pronoun, similar to the English "one," which is often how *on* is translated into English when it isn't flipped around into a passive construction. Ramuz's *on* was particular to his style, both daring and perplexing in equal measure. It clearly reflects one of the ways in which he grappled with the changes of his time period.

In *Si le soleil*, however, he wields it with more reticence than in some of his other novels, and as a result, paradoxically, the risk is higher for this to come across as a mistake in translation. Wherever possible I have tried to maintain Ramuz's ambiguity, but without being overly conspicuous. This often becomes a slightly jarring "we" depending on the context.

Aside from the POV, one other small moment bears mentioning. One of the hardest elements to translate from one language to another is a double-meaning accomplished through a homonym, and one which adds a significant layer of meaning to a scene or story. At the end of the novel, a character is called *la dorée* by another character in reference to her sun-kissed skin. In French the double-meaning is clear: *la dorée* / *l'adorée* (golden one / beloved). To my great dismay, I could not find a satisfying translation for this delightful and meaningful play on words without over-explicating it or making it awkward, and so, alas, a small example of Ramuz's flair for language is eclipsed by an altogether different kind of question—whether readers now, 80 years later and unfamiliar with his world and its preoccupations, might find something to admire and study in an English translation of his work. I hope the answer is yes.

Michelle Bailat-Jones
May 2016
Lausanne

ONE

Denis Revaz left his house that day around four thirty. He was walking with a pronounced limp.

It was his knee that was "causing the trouble"—as he liked to say; and when we asked him, "How's your knee doing?" he answered, "knee's troubling me."

In this way he struggled along the little street which crossed the village, and then we saw him heading left onto a path leading to an old house.

We could hardly discern the house in the shadow; yet we made out that it was a stone house with a roof covered in large slate shingles, and because of its color the roof blended in with the night. But is it really the night? Or is it the fog? Or something else? Because already more than fifteen days had passed since the sun had disappeared behind the mountains and would not return for another six months.

And then there was this knee that was causing trouble.

Revaz stopped a moment to let the pain subside; then, in the deepening darkness, through the open windows on the facade of the house, a russet-colored glimmer started to move like the wing of a bat.

These windows had neither shutters nor curtains, and the front of the house itself was traversed by a large crack which made it look like a notebook page crossed out with a pen; and it was at the bottom of the facade that we saw the glimmer rising, descending, appearing, disappearing, like someone shaking a faded fragment of cloth behind the panes of glass.

Which meant that Revaz was immediately assured that Anzévui

was home (besides, how would he have not been) and Revaz got himself walking again despite his ailing knee, but fortunately the path wasn't long.

He arrived in front of the porch. It was three steps on the side of the house, each with an end dug into the hillside. It was three steps which moved beneath the feet because they had gotten loose; the steps led to an old arched door. And there was no longer any handle on the door; it was a thick string which moved the lock on the inside, because everything here was old and damaged. Revaz stopped before the door, having made some noise with his large hobnailed shoes on the shale-stone steps; no one moved inside the house.

He rapped his fist against the door. "Antoine Anzévui, are you there?"

No one answered.

"It's me, Revaz. Denis Revaz. Can't I come in?"

All this time he still didn't pull on the little rope and so he had to wait until someone got up inside, and he finally heard the noise of a piece of furniture moving; then, the door having been slowly opened, something white appeared in the gap of the door.

"Oh, it's just you. What do you want?"

"I wanted to speak with you, sir."

The door was opened wide, so Revaz only had to step in.

At first, we saw nothing; then we saw that a fire was burning in the hearth.

Next we saw a large mantelpiece jutting out from the wall toward the middle of the room, and beneath it sat an old walnut table strewn with a jumble of all kinds of objects, and there was an armchair with a broken straw seat pulled between the table and the fire.

The door had closed; dragging his feet, Anzévui moved forward toward Revaz. He took a stool and placed it in front of the armchair before the fire.

"Sit there," he said; then he went back to his seat; but we saw that his seat was taken up by a large book with a red parchment binding which was worn along the spine and frayed at the edges. Anzévui picked it up carefully and with a certain respect, and then placed it face down on the table.

He had a great white beard; he had long white hair which fell about his shoulders.

"Well?" he said.

"Antoine Anzévui," said Revaz, "I'm quite sorry to disturb you. You were busy studying. You're a wise man; you read in the books. What is that? Is it the Bible?"

Anzévui was not moving.

He was holding his black hands together over his knees; and because it takes time to grow accustomed to the dim light, it was only now that we saw across to the walls, revealing that the room where we were sitting was a very big room. The glow from the fire threw a half-circle on the uneven floor tiles; from time to time it grew, reaching the windows which were cut out of the opposite wall. And so we saw that the room had once been a very beautiful room—as happens sometimes in the mountains, we find that amongst the little wooden houses sits a great stone house built by a man from the village upon his return to the area after making his fortune abroad. Only, over time, and because there wasn't enough money, the stone house is neglected; this explains why there were holes in the ceiling, and why most of the windowpanes had been replaced with parcel paper, and why the smoke from the hearth had blackened the whitewashed walls. The only white spot remaining in the room was Anzévui's hair and beard.

Anzévui was a man familiar with all kinds of illnesses; we came from far to ask for his help because he gathered medicinal plants from the mountains, and people bought his plants and his plants would heal them.

This was how Anzévui made his living; it was also why Revaz had come to see him that evening. And so he spoke again.

"Listen, Antoine Anzévui, just tell me if I'm disturbing you; I need your advice; it's my right knee that's causing me some trouble."

"What did you do to your knee?"

"I don't know," said Revaz. "I twisted it. During the second harvest. This is a while ago, you know. I must have moved it wrong... and since then, it's stayed swollen. More than that, every time I move it, it all starts again."

"Show it to me."

The other man rolled up his trouser leg. In the firelight, we saw his skinny, gray leg with knots of greenish veins, and while he pulled on the thick, brown half-wool cloth, it resisted; but he kept rolling it up.

"That's why I'm using a stick, you see, I can't go out anymore without a stick. It's a bother. I'm like an old person. Which is why I told myself to go and ask you for some advice. And so I'm asking you, Antoine Anzévui, what do you think?"

He was leaning over his knee, holding his trouser leg up on his thigh with both hands; and his knee was like a fat red beet, swelling abruptly over the articulation and changing color. Just beneath the articulation the leg became skinny again.

"Come closer," Anzévui said.

With a thrust of his lower back, Revaz shifted his stool forward, then again a bit farther since the other man stayed in his armchair, but Anzévui's beard moved forward as he stretched out his hand; and we were surprised to see how careful and delicate he was, because he had placed his finger on the injury.

"Does that hurt?"

Revaz shook his head.

Anzévui pressed harder, and then on the side. "And now?"

"A little."

Anzévui said, "It's not much. I'll give you an herbal tea. Take a good handful of the plants, put them on the fire with a cup of water and let the tea boil for a quarter of an hour. And once the liquid has reduced, spread the mixture across a cloth and while it's still hot, apply the cloth to your knee."

He got up. He reached out his hand and turned his back. We saw him place his hand into some paper sacks arranged on the edge of the table, taking out a handful of pinkish plants from one, and from another some yellow plants, and then another and another; he mixed it all in a piece of newspaper, which he twisted at the four corners.

"You can put your trouser leg back down now," he said to Revaz.

Revaz said, "How much do I owe you?"

"Wait to see how it works on you. Put a good, hot poultice on your knee each night before you go to sleep. It might take a long time, but don't get discouraged… when you run out of medicine and if your knee isn't better, just come back."

Revaz had rolled his trouser leg back down; Anzévui was seated again; and luckily there was a large pile of logs against the wall beside the chimney, because all Anzévui had to do was reach out his arm to get the fire going again; it was clear that Revaz was a little embarrassed to keep a debt when he would have preferred paying right away.

"Listen," he said, "listen, Anzévui. I'd prefer... if you don't mind."

But Anzévui didn't seem to hear him. Anzévui had taken his book up again. He had shifted himself to the side, struggling a little to pull it to him. The book appeared to be quite heavy as Anzévui placed it back across his lap. He also took a piece of paper and a pencil which were beside the book on the table; it was a piece of torn notebook paper and the stub of a carpenter's pencil—flat, wide and skinny. He wet the tip of the pencil between his lips.

"You can do math, can't you, Revaz? You're used to calculating? Okay, so how much is 8 times 237? I'm getting old, I've maybe forgotten my arithmetic."

"Oh," said Revaz, "do that in my head?"

"Here." Anzévui passed him the pencil and the piece of paper. And after a moment, Revaz said, "That makes 1896..."

"What I thought... add 41."

"1937."

"You see," said Anzévui.

He took up the paper again; he checked his own calculations. During this time Revaz tried to see what was in the book, but, because of how it was inclined and because the text was upside-down with respect to him, he could only see that the pages were divided into two columns, one printed in black and the other in red, with a lot of numbers and all kinds of symbols like crescents, spheres with a cross suspended above them, others with the cross below them, moons, circumferences and triangles.

"It's what I thought... and so 4 and 13; the 13th of 4... maybe it's already noticeable. You haven't noticed anything?"

"Noticed what?"

"About the air, the color of the air, because it's possible that it's already sick. The sky," he said. "Because it's possible it's darkening slowly... the animals, they'll be afraid... you understand? It happens somewhere near the sun... you haven't been paying attention recently, have you?"

"Well, you know that up here, for sure, we aren't so lucky."

It's true that, for them, each year near the 25th of October the sun showed itself for the last time, and only reappeared for them near the 13th of April. On the 25th of October, at noon, above the mountain to the south, there was still a trail of fire, a vague line of sparks like when someone stirs up a blaze with a stick; and then nothing for six months. Even when the sky is at its purest, the great star is too low behind the mountains and only announces its presence through a slightly paler tint to the blue of the sky, but it passes without actually appearing.

It's a village perched high in the mountain and on the northern slope; which makes it a little village without even a church; and the village hangs there, behind a first stony breast, at the foot of another stony breast which is overhung by rocky peaks. From the bottom, from the bottom of the great valley where the Rhône flows, people tell you, "You see, all the way up there?" You can't see a thing. All you see are the high, black-pointed peaks covered in copses, bearded with pine trees, spotted gray here and there by the rush of rocks which glisten with wet; cut by gorges and in other places sewn together by enormous steel tubes where the water tumbles fifteen hundred meters to propel the turbines of the electric companies at the valley floor; but you can tip your head back as far as you like, you won't see anything else. So the people tell you, "More to the right. There where the mountain juts forward because of the valley behind it. Just on the ridge, you see. There's a notch in the ridge. Look there..." Between the crowns of the pine trees

7

stretched out like the teeth of a saw, you end up seeing a little gray spot that, at first, can be confused with the earth and surrounding fields; these are the shake-shingle roofs which take their color from the rock. There are barely a hundred residents of Upper Saint-Martin—which doesn't even have a church so that everyone walks down to Lower Saint-Martin for mass; in winter the village is practically cut off from the world, and all throughout the winter it's completely cut off from the sun because of the height of the mountain.

"And so," said Anzévui, "what we need is to be sure we won't be cut off from it forever."

"No, we're not so lucky up here," said Revaz, "but, you know, we just have to be patient."

"Only you did the math and came up with the same answer as I did... and well, I'm going to tell you since you didn't understand. Well, the book talks about a war—and right now there's a war going on. But there's also a war up there near the sun. 1896 and 41, that's how it adds up. It's also written in the book that the sky will grow darker and darker, and then one day we won't see the sun again, not just for six months, but forever."

Revaz asks, "Just us?"

"For the whole world."

A small wind began to blow. It came down the chimney where it made the ashes twirl with the smoke as it pushed out a kind of long sigh.

A small wind began to blow. It passed beneath the door, making the paper sacks on the table move and crinkle; it passed over the roof where it shifted some little round stones and we could hear them roll down the length of the slope.

And Revaz said, "Ahh."

And Revaz said, "I didn't understand so well. You study in the books. It's written in your books that the sun won't come back?" He seemed both afraid and incredulous; he was a fairly fat man, about fifty years old. "Look, it isn't possible. It's been turning and turning for so long."

"We'll see."

"For all this time it's been used to us and we've been used to it. In winter, it leaves us, I know, but it's just for a while; it doesn't really leave us, it just goes farther away..."

"It will go completely away."

"We're friends with the sun and it's useful for us."

"Well, we're going to have to learn to live without it."

"And so? It'll be dark?"

"Exactly," said Anzévui, "It's a disruption in the stars. A sickness in the stars. What can we do? It's written. Only," he said, "the calculations have to be correct. I was wondering if I hadn't made a mistake. Until we did them both together."

He said to Revaz, "Do you want to count again?"

Two

Revaz went home, and after dropping the package of plants on the kitchen table he said to his wife, "Put a handful of them in a cup of water and then boil that for half an hour. It's for my knee."

"Where have you been?"

"To Anzévui." Then he said, "And Lucien, where is he?"

"You know where he is."

"Oh!" he said. "This isn't the time for courting; I'll have to have a word with him…"

And Revaz's wife would have liked to ask him more about it, but he'd already gone out through the door.

Lucien was his son, and he had a girlfriend; and Revaz had said, "It's not the right time." He went out, it was dark; the daylight had completely gone. The last glimmers of light had finally gone out on the summit of the mountain, there where the sun sets without us being able to see it here in the village, but it usually marks itself along the peak in red spots like traces of blood on a cloth. That evening, the sky was a uniform black. Yet here and there, on the front of the houses, at a small window or at a row of little windows all stacked one on top of the another in a line, the lamplight roughly indicated the direction of the street; without which we would have been like the blind and completely unable to guide ourselves along; also because not a sound could be heard, nothing at all, because the villagers were closed up in their houses and had put between us all the thickness of a well closed door, the thickness of their double windows. It's a little street, about fifty meters long at the most, where many paths come to their end, twining between the little haybarns and what are called *raccards*, which are a kind of shed to store provisions; there are about a hundred buildings, twenty or so inhabited, and most of those border the street. Some of them have two or even three stories, and are built out of a lovely larch wood on a foundation of whitewashed stone, but the buildings were the color of shadows and of night, further deepening the darkness.

Revaz walked forward slowly, carefully, because of his hurt knee, making a soft thud with his cane in the middle of this little village which one could say has been squeezed between two hands to reduce its volume before placing it up high in the mountain, beyond the world. Usually it made a little round spot; at this time of evening, no one would even know it existed without the window of Pralong's café.

In the café were several electric lamps which shone brightly on the wooden resin-polished walls and on the four tables between which stood Fat Sidonie who had just been drying her hands on her apron.

Several lamps, a wireless, four tables; and, through an open door was the kitchen that served as a bar.

Sidonie was laughing because of a woman's voice coming out of the polished wooden box with its leaf-shaped cut-outs, covered inside with a thin metal grill (is it to keep the flies out?) while the men were listening with a serious look on their faces; there were six of them.

"...toi, tu t'la mettras sur la tête,
moi, je m'la mets dans l'estomac."

It was finished.

Revaz placed his cane in a corner. Another loud voice made itself heard; a nasally voice; and then Morand was saying, "He's got a cold." It was a conference on Chinese music.

The men turned toward Revaz; they said to him, "How are you?"

Morand, Follonnier, Lamon, Antide: Ernest Morand, Placide Follonnier, Erasme Lamon, Augustin Antide; with Revaz that made four older men and a young one; and there was yet another whose face we didn't see because he was holding it tilted down toward the table on which his arms were stacked.

"Your knee still not working?" Follonnier asked.

"Not so well."

"I know what it is; how old are you?"

"Fifty-one."

"Well, it's just age." Follonier continued, "It's not an illness. It's that we wear down. People are like tools that have been overused; there's always a spot that rubs more than another."

Revaz sat down with a sigh.

"Our knees, you know, they carry us; knees are the hinges. And in a country like ours, with nothing but hills and valleys, those hinges are working hard. Pain settles into the places that work the most. For drinkers, it's the elbow, you know. For cheapskates, it's the guts."

He was talking and laughing a lot. He was a good-natured man and Fat Sidonie was enjoying it; but Revaz kept a worried face, having not even looked at Follonnier, only saying to him, "I wanted to see you."

And Arlettaz was there, saying nothing.

This was how they were at Pralong's café, finding themselves together like they often did in winter when the nights are long; after five o'clock no one can see a thing anywhere and even before five when it's cloudy as it had been today. So they're there from six to nine and eat their dinner after if they feel like it. But the wine is nourishing, so much so that the women don't even wait for them; most often the men find them already gone to sleep when they return, lying themselves down beside the women in the big bed for one more night—which makes one less night to live, like tearing a page from a book that doesn't have many pages left.

For now they are at Pralong's, talking of their business and drinking a liter or two of Muscat. They are discussing the price of mules and of cows, if they're up or if they're down, if it's better to sell or maybe to buy; discussing the quality of the second sowing, of the lending rates, of the next elections, of news of the war, because there are always wars (that year there was one in Spain); and right now, because of the wireless telegraph, from time to time they quieted down to listen to the news.

It's a voice that comes from who knows where, born from nowhere or everywhere, born of nothing, the offspring of emptiness. It's music, violins, trumpets, drums; it's a woman, a crowd, thundering canons, firing rifles, ten thousand men or only one, the sound of the wind, the sound of the waves. And at first this sound was something, but now it's nothing for us, only sound. The ear no longer distinguishes where it begins. A sound with a varying intensity but without meaning in terms of the distance it has traveled. The leagues do not make it tired, it's not bothered by the myriameters; in this way it might be weak when it says, "This is Geneva," or strong but it's coming from New York. On the mountain the echo splits the sounds, and as they echo they cross, making the sound bounce off the opposite wall where it was thrown; but one's eyes tell you immediately where it was coming from, because we are ourselves a reality in a world that is also a real thing; — here, in this café, at first the customers tried to lean over the box, looking to understand through the openings how it worked inside and to understand the thing of it; they quickly saw there was nothing to see, no spools, no gears, no record, no needles, nothing but bulbs, and it was Fat Sidonie who decided with a simple flick of her fingers which country was going to come through: a woman like us; so that having experienced the miracle, they accepted it at the same time.

They were no longer listening to what was being said on the wireless, which was like a faucet that we turned on in the morning.

It was Revaz we were listening to, because he had finally started to answer Follonnier. He was saying, "I came to find you. Look at this for me." He turned his knee toward Follonnier. "Just touch, it's like a baby's head. I can hardly bend the leg."

"It's rheumatism," said Lamon.

"Rheumatism? I've got that in my shoulder, it doesn't swell, and yet this knee gets bigger and bigger throughout the day, it gets heavier, it heats up...so..."

We saw he had something to say, and he was hesitating to say it. Then he couldn't not say it, "And so, well, I ended up going to ask Anzévui for some advice."

Follonnier burst out laughing.

"And he gave you some of his plants?"

"Yes, some compresses to do each evening."

"For sure."

"He's an educated man," Lamon said.

"Yes, he makes sure to take advantage of people."

"He's an educated man," Morand said.

"He knows things that the rest of us don't know," Revaz was saying.

Arlettaz still wasn't saying anything.

"He studies in those big books."

And Augustin was listening and Revaz said, "And well, when I found him, he was in the middle of reading in one of his books, he was doing some calculations..."

"Calculations about what?" asked Follonnier.

"Calculations about the sun."

Then Follonnier began to laugh even more, and the others grew attentive, while Fat Sidonie, drawn by the noise, reappeared at the door to the kitchen.

"Anyway," said Follonnier, "he always knew how to get himself business. He's never had a penny, but he knows how to get some from all of you, even if none of you parts easily with your cash. He's been lucky that the world is half made for women, eh? With his plants and his teas..."

"It isn't that," Revaz said.

"And there have been girls who were worried at the end of their month..."

"It isn't that."

"What is it?"

"It's the sun."

"The sun?"

"Yes."

"And what's going to happen to the sun?"

"Nothing good," said Revaz.

He had brought his knee back to him, holding it stretched out beneath the table and he took his glass, and his other leg was bent at a right angle; he emptied his glass in one gulp as if to give himself some courage; everyone was watching him, except Arlettaz, and everyone was turned toward him:

"Well, he said that the sun doesn't have much light left for those of us up here. He's done his calculating. He says the calculations say 1937, and they say four and thirteen. That gives no more than four or five months. And then he says 'gone'."

"Who's going to be gone? Anzévui?"

"No, the sun."

Follonnier tapped a hand on his leg. But at the same time, Arlettaz had lifted his big head with its small eyes. "All the better," he said.

"Why?"

"I won't have to look for her anymore…"

"You're crazy," Follonnier yelled, "you're crazy, Arlettaz. Although not as much as Revaz, and he's not as crazy as Anzévui, we can say that for sure! So, be quiet," he said, "because Revaz hasn't finished explaining…"

He tapped his thigh again, "So, about this sun?"

"Well, I don't know; I'm not an educated man like Anzévui. I haven't read his books…"

"We're only asking you to tell us how it's going to happen, this business of the sun losing its light. How will it lose its light?"

"I don't know; it's going out, or maybe we're going to stop turning…"

"Oh, but that's just it," Follonnier said, "we're turning and we can't stop turning. How do you want us to stop turning?"

"I don't know."

"We're even turning twice, because we're turning around the sun and then we're turning around ourselves, and that's what makes day and night. For us to have nothing but the night, we'd have to be like the moon."

"Exactly…"

"Or maybe the sun will break up into pieces; how can it break up into pieces? It'd have to hit a comet."

"Exactly."

"But there are no comets… or maybe it grows cold suddenly and turns black like when somebody pisses on a fire…"

But a louder voice came onto the wireless right then: *Events in Spain. The nationals are nearing Malaga. One of the detachments is advancing along the sea route, the other has just arrived at the city through the mountains… The taking of Malaga seems to be but a question of days.*

Which encouraged Revaz:

"He told me (talking of Anzévui) that there would be a war and that before the end of the war, the sun would turn itself away from us. And that's all I know but I wanted to warn you all, because, if by chance what Anzévui has said is right, it wouldn't be bad to know about it beforehand. There might be some precautions to take."

"My poor friend, what precautions?"

"I don't know, lock yourself at home, gather provisions."

"You'd be frozen right away, old chap."

"Yes, but if we had enough wood, we could wait…"

"What for what?"

"For the sun to come back."

"Well…" said Arlettaz, "I hope it doesn't come back. It'd be good for me if it didn't come back."

He'd been looking all over the country for his daughter for the last two years, a tall beautiful girl of 19 who had left the house; and she had left a note on the kitchen table saying she'd gone to her cousin's house in Sion. And Arlettaz had gone to the cousin's two weeks later to see her and she was no longer there.

The cousin had laughed, "Oh, she didn't stay here long; no way of keeping her."

"And where is she?"

"I don't know."

So Arlettaz had begun looking for his daughter everywhere, leaving his house for weeks on end and reappearing again suddenly; he'd gone to one end of the country, on the German side, and all the way to the Rhône Glacier: he hadn't found her. Then, on the other side, to beyond Saint Maurice: just as futile; — meanwhile now he turned toward us with a wrinkled face and from within its great beard, with his two tiny stunned eyes: "I'd finally get some rest; and not just for my legs," he said, "because it isn't just one's legs that get tired, it's the spirit, from always being forced to think and imagine…"

Because it was nearly three years; and his head fell down again.

Follonier shrugged his shoulders twice, but he was maybe the only one who was really steady, a vague uneasiness having taken over everyone who was there, including Augustin. And Augustin said, "Well, it must be said that the weather has been strange this winter."

He was a young man.

"Don't you all think? For the last month or two, since we haven't had the sun… but that's normal. What isn't, well, it's this fog, this ceiling over our heads. Maybe Anzévui is right; maybe the sun is weakening…"

"Look," said Follonier, "we shouldn't forget to drink; what do you say, Arlettaz, you're a man who doesn't like the taste of water…"

But they didn't seem to be listening to him and even Fat Sidonie at the edge of the kitchen had turned toward Augustin. They were answering him:

"I just don't know, maybe so."

Morand was saying, "All that I know is that Anzévui is a learned man and more than a little… And, after all, what he's saying, you know, his predictions…"

"I'm also thinking it's possible," Lamon was saying, "and maybe even likely, even if it's never happened, but I'm telling you he's a wise man…"

Ladies and Gentlemen, here is tomorrow's weather forecast: Uncertain conditions… Rain in the lowlands, fog in the mountains… low temperatures… sun spots may be the cause of these unseasonal conditions.

"You hear that," said Revaz. "Sun spots."

"Huh? Sun spots…" said Arlettaz.

All this time she was waiting for her husband, listening out for him; they'd only been married six months.

This was Isabelle Antide, Augustin's wife. She was waiting for him in their bedroom, which was walled with lovely new larch planks, with the electric light and its pink-pearl lampshade around the light bulb.

She was sitting in a chair next to the big bed that was covered in a garnet-colored lace coverlet, which had been a wedding present from her friends; she was wondering what he could be doing.

Right then at Pralong's, Augustin wanted to get up from his bench; we all said to him: "You're in a rush."

She was waiting next to the big bed and on the walls surrounding her was their entire family in large or small photographic portraits: her mother in a black gold filigree frame, a cousin who was a policeman, a cousin who was an army sergeant, a cousin who worked for the railroad, all three of them in uniform; and there was also a painting of St. Cecilia in a blue satin gown with her beautiful hands raised to her face, her fingers half-threaded through the strings of her instrument.

It was a concert harp.

Augustin stood up again at Pralong's; we all told him, "Wait a minute."

But then Follonier started to laugh: "Let him go! We all know why he's in such a hurry."

We let Augustin leave.

The rest of the men in the café went back to their discussion; he—the young man—was for a moment in the darkness, then the door of the bedroom had opened on its own at the top of the wooden staircase because she—Isabelle—was behind it; and she greeted him beneath the lamplight with the light of her eyes.

"Oh, there you are! Finally!"

But immediately she continued, "What's wrong?"

A little house had been built for them next to the older one where his parents lived—Mr. and Mrs. Antide; it had been built just for the two of them last summer, with a bedroom and a kitchen on the ground floor, and two rooms upstairs.

"Nothing's wrong."

"But there is," she said, "I can tell something isn't right."

"It's just that he's a wise man," he said.

Her face was like a ripe peach.

"Who is such a wise man?"

She had taken him around the neck; she had made him tumble into the chair; she had sat on his knees.

Augustin said, "He reads in the books."

And she said, "Who do you mean?"

"Anzévui."

"And so?"

"Well," he said, "it won't last much longer, because everything is going to end."

"When?"

"Soon."

But she let him go. She started to laugh. "You ninny!" she said. "Come on, Augustin, come on, are you really going to believe this kind of story? I know your Anzévui pretty well! When we were little, about four or five of us went up once to the Chassoures Woods to get flowers for the Corpus Christi; he was there. You know he's always collecting his plants; we saw from afar that he was looking for them, but he didn't see us. This is maybe ten years ago; he wasn't as old as he is now. He still had a beard, but not as long and not as white as it was now; he wasn't so badly dressed either, even if we were already afraid of him. We hid behind the trees. And then farther up was Brigitte, Old Brigitte, but she wasn't so old either, and she was collecting wood. Do you know what Anzévui did? He called to her, but she didn't want to go to him. He was saying things to her, all kinds of things, he was saying, 'Come on, come here, no one will bother us.' But she stuck her tongue out at him. So we all started to laugh, we were laughing so hard that Ambroisine Pralong told us to hush because he would hear us. And then he was chasing after Brigitte, who had scampered off; only she had a head start. So you be quiet," she said. "You just be quiet."

And she silenced him with her mouth because she could see Augustin wanted to start talking again. She put her lips on his lips, then: "So that's all he is, your Anzévui. He's nothing but a man, and not a very honest one. You know, Ambroisine Pralong, she went to see him not too long ago. She was having dizzy spells; she told him she didn't know what it was. He said to her, 'Ambroisine, you've been with the boys.' Oh, she was laughing so hard telling me about her visit. She said, 'if only that were the truth, oh, if only it was that.' You know she'll be 24 soon. She told me, 'Oh no, he wasn't very smart... God knows, however, if I wanted... but you never know what might happen...' So you be quiet! Be quiet!" she said.

And she quieted him, yes; then, "What do we care about these stories, anyway? He's so old now, he's so very old, he's going to die. He hasn't paid the rent on his house for some time now; it's falling in on his head; one of these days the house will fall down. Maybe he's talking about his house or about himself, because it won't last much longer..."

She said to him, "So you be quiet!"

She placed a kiss on one eye, and then on the other one. She said to him, "Your cheeks are so soft today, you're well-shaven."

She placed a kiss on each cheek.

And another kiss a bit lower, so that he couldn't say another thing, he could only shake his head; eventually he lost the power to do even that.

THREE

Sometime after that, Denis Revaz's eldest son came home to visit his parents from where he had been working in the vineyards along the lake. He came home on Saturday night; and then on Sunday, as is the custom, he went visiting around the households with whom he was friendly.

And so around two o'clock, he showed up at Augustin Antide's house. Augustin was somehow a distant cousin.

We asked him to sit down. We asked him, "How did you come?"

"With the goods truck."

"To where?"

"Just to Lower Saint-Martin."

"There wasn't too much snow?"

"Well," he said, "but they've got a good truck and a good driver; he's an Italian. He goes everywhere, in all weather. But what a strange place our village is; such a sad place."

"And what about down there?"

"It's all gray up here; down there it's blue. We had wonderful weather this year all through the grape harvest. Up here, there's no sun for the entire winter, down there they've got two suns all year long. That makes a difference, you see."

We said to him, "Two?"

"Yes, there's the one in the sky and also the one in the water."

We said to him, "The one in the water?"

"Yes, because of the lake. Oh, it's steep down there, it's even steeper than up here. It's this hillside along the water, it's like the side of a bathtub that is 200 meters high. And the earth wouldn't stay in place by itself, so they've made these walls everywhere, they've stacked them one on top of the other to hold it in place; and that's where they grow their grapes and use their hand hoes, each winter using their grape baskets to carry the soil that's rolled down. It's like they're standing on stair steps, you see, standing in the air because the air is everywhere. Above them is the blue air, in front of them the blue mountain, below them the blue lake. The sun beats on your head, but there's another one, the one below, that beats against your back. That makes two: the one above, which is a fixed point, held together; and the one below which is broken up and scattered into little pieces because of the water that throws it back against the lakeshore; that makes two suns heating at the same time: which is why they have such good wine."

"So you're happy down there?"

"Well," said Julien Revaz, "not so much, you know. I miss home... or at least not so much until yesterday, and I was happy to come home..."

"And now you're not happy anymore?"

"Oh," he says, "it's the change in weather. It was sunny until Sion."

"And from Sion?"

"Well, you see... because I found the truck in Sion, and it was sunny up until the Rhône. But at that point there was a bar across the lowlands; it was the shadow of the mountains. And until then there was no snow, but then everything went white. At the same time the air changed, the color of the air, the color of things, because there's no sun here. And there's no lake either to mirror the sun."

"It's true it's gray this year," said Augustin's father.

"So," said Julien Revaz, "We climbed up; the road was open until Lower Saint-Martin, but the truck just barely passed through; there was a good meter of snow on each side of the road. It was a good thing, too," he said, "because we were sliding, but he's a good driver.

I asked him what he was carrying, and he told me he had macaroni, rice, some herrings for Lent, sugar, a bag of coffee. What's difficult were the curves; he told me not to look but I raised my head and you know, there was nothing, no Devil's Horn, no Dents Rouges, no Grimpion: nothing except for what looked like a vaulted ceiling with water stains."

"It's true it's really cloudy this year," said Augustin's mother.

"And what's hard," said Julien Revaz, "is that there isn't time to get used to it, you know, to these differences, these changes. It all goes too fast. I still had the lake in my head and the vineyards; my head was still full of the flowers in the cracks of the vineyard walls: so, well, you feel yourself slide to the side, lean over, look to where you've leaned, and you see that you're above this emptiness. This was where the road turns at Goillettes, and there, you know, you're just above the Serine gorge; you all know it, there where the rock juts out; it's a 300 meter sheer drop. But it wasn't just the drop that worried me, it was that it was so gray, the weather was so gloomy... Luckily, we arrived with no problems to Lower Saint-Martin and we found something to drink."

"Well," said Isabelle, "You just need something else to drink. Up here our sun comes in the bottle... Hey, Augustin..."

Augustin went to get a bottle and glasses.

"We keep our sun in the wine cellar, we don't have to go far to find it."

They drank; someone asked Julien Revaz how things were at his house.

"That's the thing, not so well."

"Not so well?"

"No, not really, my father is complaining about his knee. And my brother, well, you know he's courting, but even there we don't really know what's going on, because my father is angry. My father says it isn't the time to think of getting married; so Lucien has to see his girl in secret, and no one's happy."

He looked around him.

"There's no color in their faces, and, all of you, well, it's true there isn't much color in your faces either; everyone is so pale. Yes, you, Mr. Antide, and you, Mrs. Antide, and you, too, Augustin."

"And me?" said Isabelle.

"Oh, not you!"

"And me?" said Augustin's brother, Jean.

"Oh, not you. And how is it," he asked, "that there would be such a difference, since you're all living in the shadow? Is it age? But you're not old Augustin. If you came from where I'm coming from, you'd have the sun written across your face, because it'll continue, it lasts, we don't know what winter is down there; over the winter the sun unites the time when the vine leaves are yellow with the time when the trunks weep and dampen the ground beneath them, because so much water drips from the pruned wood..."

Was it because he'd already drunk so much? But he was off, and they couldn't stop him. "Over the winter it unites autumn and spring."

"Listen," said Augustin.

"Over the winter it unites the ripe grapes to the green grapes; what will you do without it?"

"That's exactly..."

Isabelle had grasped Augustin by the sleeve. It didn't stop him, "You don't know yet, there's some news... it seems that there won't..."

Isabelle put her hand on his mouth, but he moved quickly backward, "The sun..."

His voice was stifled once again, he started again: "It's Anzévui, he's wise you know…"

Now he held Isabelle by her wrists. "He says that the sun won't come back, and that it's been written in the books."

"So you believe these stories?" said Julien Revaz. "It's doesn't surprise me if you'd believe them, a place like ours, a poor place, a sad place, a place where it goes away for six months. This gives you ideas."

"And I saw him," said Brigitte. "I saw Anzévui."

She had been there for a while but no one had paid her any attention. She was all dressed in black, with a black kerchief knotted around her head, and as she was seated a little behind everyone in a corner, her small person was easily confused with the shadows.

We asked her, "You saw him?"

"Sure, I went to see him."

"And what did he tell you?"

"He said that it was written…."

"And you believe him?"

"Yes, I believe."

What was surprising was that at that exact instant, Julian Revaz stood up. We said to him, "What are you doing?"

"I'm going."

"But you've got plenty of time. You said you were planning to stay until tomorrow."

"I've changed my mind."

"How will you manage to go back? You won't be foolish enough to take the road at night?"

"I'll manage things. Good bye! Maybe I'll see you next spring."

FOUR

"The sun will vomit red, and then it won't be there anymore."

This is what Anzévui had said to Old Brigitte and she scared the women by telling them what Anzévui had told her.

"He asked me to come do his housekeeping, you understand. He's getting old, you see? He has trouble walking, he's coughing, he's run too much in his life, he's tired. He's there beneath his plants; if you ever want anything…"

They said to her, "Yes, maybe…if ever…"

"He's there beneath his plants; sometimes he's coughing, sometimes he isn't coughing. It was when he went roaming all over the mountain; he made bouquets out of them, you see? He hung them from the ceiling, head down."

"Yes," she said, "with strings—from the rafters and with strings. There are some that make you sweat; there are some that are good for the lungs; others, for the stomach. Well, they're a little old, that's for sure, his plants, but if you want any… And it won't cost you anything."

"Oh, thank you…"

"Only you'll need to hurry, because there are only three months left… And I think he'll pass on when the sun does. He says that he'll go out just like the sun, soft and slow, because the sun will leave us little by little, and he'll also leave us little by little."

"And all the better for him," she said, "because there are those who will have to let go all at once."

Justine Emonet had just had a child: "It isn't fair!"

She held the baby in her arms; it was a sugar child, a sugar child because it was wrapped up so tightly in a white woolen blanket; she took from his face the white handkerchief she'd used to cover it because of the cold.

"But just look at his lovely complexion. And he's smart, he already knows how to laugh. Is it at all fair that we have to finish before we've even gotten started?"

Then, in the icy air, she leaned over the little warm round spot in the crook of her left arm; she pressed her lips to the spot, she couldn't unpress them.

Brigitte continued, "He told me he still had a little money in the drawer. That will be enough, I said. I told him he doesn't need much anymore, maybe a bit of cheese. And he said he had some."

"'And some bread,' I said, and he told me he had some of that too but it was dry, he'd have to soak it, so I told him I would soak it, make him some bread soup. That's how we arranged things, that I would do his shopping and sometimes I'd go and make up his bed and do a little sweeping."

Just then we saw Cyprien Métrailler go into the house belonging to his friend Tissières. The day was still sad and the clouds hanging low.

There was no more sky; there was only a yellowish fog stretching from one slope to the other, like an old washrag, a little above the village, and with the mountains behind—or do they really still exist? All those peaks and squares and rounds, those that are like towers, the ones like horns, the ones made out of boulders, made out of ice—did they once shine all together in the blue sky?

Métrailler found Tissières warming himself at his fire. Métrailler sat down beside Tissières.

"I'm bored. And you?"

"I'm bored, too."

"Well, you should come with me then."

"Where to?"

"You've got to come with me to try to go find the sun, somewhere above the Bisse forests. Between the two of us, I'll be damned if we can't shoot a goat, because they must be lower down right now."

They were old friends, they always hunted together, and not always when it was hunting time, but all year long; and they'd never had permits, which saves some money of course, but which is also good for mocking the government.

They knew all of the mountain's nooks and crannies by heart, all its passages, its hideaways, all of which meant they didn't have to worry too much about the hunting warden.

Only that day Tissières shook his head.

Métrailler said to him: "Why?"

"There's too much snow."

"It'll carry our weight," said Métrailler.

"What do you know about it?"

"There was a hard freeze these last few nights."

"Yes, but the wind."

"There was hardly any wind."

"And it's such strange weather..."

Tissières stretched an arm toward the window.

It was actually brownish outside, between the chinks of the windows with their little panes of glass; everywhere it was all brown and sad, with a singular lack of movement to the air, so much so that the daylight hardly made its way into the room.

"The weather," Métrailler said, "what do you think it might bother with us, this weather?"

"The fog…"

"This isn't fog. Besides, you're acting like this is the first time we're heading out when it's cloudy…"

But Tissières didn't want to get into it. He didn't even answer; he just shook his head. Métrailler didn't recognize his friend.

And he said, "Oh, well, too bad, I'll go anyway. That doesn't stop me. I want to go find the sun… because it hides too long for us when we stay closed up in the village; and it's stupid, because a person's got legs."

He kept on, "And also I'm bored, and I can tell you're bored too, only you don't want to admit it."

Tissières still wouldn't answer. So Métrailler took his leave.

He lived with his old father who had grown nearly blind in his old age. Old Man Métrailler no longer saw the shapes of things, only the vague light they gave off; he could see nothing anymore but what was dark and what was light; and for some time now he'd been saying, "Is everything getting more gray, because it's all starting to look the same."

People told him, "It's that there isn't any more sun."

People told him, "You've got to wait. Nothing has any color when it isn't being lit up. Just be patient; and the day will surely come when we can bring you a bouquet of gentians and a bouquet of primroses; you'll see the difference right away, you'll see. And it'll be soon, Mr. Métrailler."

Meanwhile young Métrailler had prepared his rifle. It was a cavalry carbine which is a shorter and lighter weapon compared to the infantry rifle. A long-barreled rifle is difficult among the rocks; a too-heavy rifle would be uncomfortable, as it isn't always easy to get into the right position among the gravelly rocks where a body can't get down on the knees or stay standing or stretch out, where most often one has to shoot with a stretched arm and a guess. He also prepared all that he would need for the next day in terms of clothes and food; and now, by lamplight, close to two o'clock in the afternoon, he was busy oiling his weapon. He had completely disassembled the bolt and its pieces were spread out in front of him on the table, each one placed on a square of cloth, because he was a careful man; then, taking his carbine by the small end, he held it in such a way that the lamplight (because usually one would use the sun, but there was no longer any sun) was just in front of him on the other side of the barrel. And, again, he passed the cord into the barrel until he had removed even the slightest spot on the steel where the light must be like a taut continuous line of silver.

No one saw him leave the next morning because it was not even six o'clock.

He had been very careful as he woke not to make the bed creak. He had managed to place his feet on the floorboards so as to remain perfectly silent, which was not easy, because of the length of the boards and how their age made them shift and because they were simply nailed to the cross beams that separated them from the rooms below, without any plaster insulation. He had gotten dressed silently; he had gone down the wooden staircase, barefoot, stopping on each step; in this way he made it to the door; once there he held himself still for a moment. But nothing was moving in the house and nothing could be heard but the regular soft beating of an old grandfather clock. He aligned himself with its ticking to turn the key in the lock, to pull the heavy door to him, to close it behind him.

He saw then that there was nothing to see around him or at least he could see nothing, as if he himself had lost his vision. He had to feel with his hands to find the bench placed against the wall of the house, in the shelter of the front roof. He sat there to put on his shoes. Then all he had to do was stretch his leg so that his foot met with a good thickness of snow; so that he had nothing to worry about anymore for the noise; but it was so dark and this bothered him. Métrailler raised his head, it seemed he didn't even raise it; he turned his head to the side, it seemed to him that he didn't even turn it, the heights were completely hidden, the depths and the distance, too; meanwhile he swore in the name of Tissières, scornful of what his friend was doing. Sleeping? Well, he would go anyway, he thought, even if inside him he heard a small whispered voice, *you won't get through this on your own, Cyprien, it'd be better to stay put where you are.*

He set out. He had to hold one foot to the side to feel the location and the direction of the path through the sole of his shoe. In this way he brought himself to the road, followed it from one end to the other. At the end he arrived in front of what was, in normal weather, a wide vista opening out onto the valley, a broad view of high mountains, pastures, forests, rocks, névé snow packs, lonely glaciers with double-sided slopes which meet up again at the base of the mountain; but there was nothing there in the perfection of the night. There was no more color, the night being only the negation of all that is; all that remained was a weak glimmer, something like an emanation or a vague phosphorescence.

He walked forward anyway, not listening at all to the voice of caution which kept telling him not to go, even if he had to shoot a goat, even if he had to shoot two of them. The voice asked him if it wouldn't be better to be sure he could carry it back down on his back? Wouldn't it be better to be sure he was able to bring himself back down?

Obstinately, he went on, holding his eyes fixed just in front of him, raising them little by little as they adjusted, taking first nothing from what they saw, then one thing or another; and a separation grew between the things that were down below and the things that were up above, between the ground and the air, between that which resists your advance and that which concedes to it, making appear in front of him a low wall here, a hedge over there, then a copse of larch—because of which he recognized that he was going in the right direction. He walked up across the hill that overlooks the village. It must be said that the snow carried his weight easily. It must be said that it slowly became distinct from the night to which it served as a base. Métrailler could now see his feet and even his hand when he stretched out his arm, being warmly and thoroughly equipped (he's a hunter), supplied with food and drink, armed as well, with his carbine hanging at the shoulder, his legs wrapped in his fleece lined puttees, his head and ears in his hood with its two straps tied under his chin. All this encouraged his resolve. And, as long as he moved forward, he kept separating out the contrary elements; he reconstructed the world as it should be, as it was going to be, imagining the daylight before it came, advancing the day with his impatient eyes. The great winds from the mountain had not blown for awhile on their land, having remained closed up in their caves. Because of this the snow was equal in its thickness and consistency, compared to when it's otherwise chased and harried about, becoming like sand in a desert and piling up into the folds of the ground while leaving the rises bare. Everywhere the snow was covered in a thin layer of ice, no thicker than a plate of glass, easily broken beneath the foot with the sound of a pebble thrown against a window; Métrailler left footprints behind him that were as clear as if they had been cut with scissors in cardboard. And he knew where he was at each step because of objects he expected, one after the other, that appeared and were so well known to him: there was a cross, and a large stone, and he left the cross waiting to see the stone appear in front of him, and then it was a larch standing on its own. And then he saw the village appear; and the white on white village would have been nothing at all if there hadn't been the black wood of the house fronts, which, seen from above and to the side, were like holes in the snow, as if water had flooded the snowfall. And the night was retreating and he was the one to make it retreat. He held his arm forward; he saw that with this gesture the daylight was slowly awakened. And he said, "Yes, there it is! And they're all dead down there because they've agreed to be dead. They have lain down together in that bad air beneath a duvet, beneath a ceiling, beneath a roof, and then beneath one more layer—the snow—and a third roof that is the night; well, I'm going to look for the light because I'm still alive. I'm going to bring them the sun that has left them; and, for the moment, I'm making the light again." Because he believed that he was making it come alive above the village—even if it was still small and hesitant. He waved to the village, then he lost sight of the village almost immediately. He stepped out onto a ridge that rose above the hill he had just passed. Here, in normal weather, it feels like stepping onto a stiff rope. It's a place where two inclines meet up, finding that their summits coincide; it's not a large path, suspended in the air, a place where, in normal weather, there is a magnificent view of the deserts of glaciers and rocks perched on high; but that morning there was nothing else but this little bit of snow and several rounded rocks across a space of a few meters in front of him. And turning around, he could only see several meters behind him, and nothing else. A vague and limitless immensity of light fog, if it was truly fog and not a simple blocking of the daylight. Because the day had risen a little, although now it was no longer rising; it was immobile and somehow knotted up on itself. Métrailler took his watch from his pocket; he saw that it was eight o'clock. And he pushed himself forward. He could see well enough to direct himself, even if there were no other landmarks except those that were found in his immediate proximity, but they were enough for him—because we know you, O mountain, we know you and your tiniest details; you're like a woman with whom we have slept for a long time; there is no spot, not the slightest flaw nor the smallest beauty mark on your skin that we have not touched at least once with a finger or our lips. This is how you are for me, he was thinking; go ahead and blow out the light, I do not need a candle. I'm going to follow the ridge to the base of the Vire rocks, and then, using the passage, I'll arrive at Grand-Dessus. Up there a person is above everything. And even if the devil gets mixed up in it, he can't stop the sun from paying me a visit; I'll bring it back to everyone down below, a little bit in my pocket; I'll tell them that it still exists, because they will end up doubting this... and I'll surely get a goat as I pass across. I will bring them back the sun in my pockets, the goat on my back.

Indeed, this was the time of year when the chamois leave their high summer pastures to descend into the lower valleys where they scratch at the snow with their sharp little hooves to find the moss beneath. Yes, they go down into the forest, and sometimes all the way to the hay barns where they eat the hay that sticks out beyond the spaces between the beams. Métrailler checked one more time that the six cartridges in his magazine were well in place, and he had a seventh in the barrel of his rifle; now there was nothing to do but wait until the view opened up, which is what he was thinking would be the case when he had made it just a bit higher up the mountain.

He had now moved beyond the ridge to his left, slipping down into its trench. Pulled down by its own weight, the snow had hardly held to the heights of the scree of slim gravel and tiny rocks that Métrailler had begun to walk across and which was bare in places, having hardened and stuck together with the ice. He moved along without too much trouble; meanwhile, a kind of round half-lit room was also moving along, and he moved forward in the middle of it while it moved forward around him. And now because he had stopped, the noise he was making with his boots and his breath suddenly grew quiet; and, overlooking the secret expanse— he had imagined it, saw it in his mind—now came to him through its silence and in which he could hear nothing but the sound of his heart. It came, he listened; from beneath his heavy brown jacket came those regular beats which were like the ticking of a watch behind his ribs. Nothing else was alive, nothing behind him nor in front of him, nor to his left or to his right, or as far as he could imagine; and that voice could be heard again: *Go back to where you came from, Métrailler. If you slip, there'll be no one to rescue you; if you get lost, who will hear you? If you break a leg, what will you do, Métrailler? It only takes one false move, Métrailler; there's ice on these rocks.* But he shook his head as if to say no, having made it all the way across the rock flow to the base of the wall where the passage that led to Grand-Dessus could be found.

Climbing up through the corridor was long and difficult. He dug holes with the tips of his shoes into the frozen snow and using these holes, moving from one to the next, he climbed from the bottom, holding on with his fingers into the hard crust like holding onto the rungs of a ladder.

He kept telling himself that the sun was above him. And, indeed, it seemed that the sun must show itself soon, because above Métrailler was a thinning of the clouds like a cloth whose weave has loosened. And, on the other side of the ridge, a reddish tint had begun to appear. Métrailler raised his head and, growing prideful now with his solitude, said, "I'll show Tissières, I'll show everyone!" He arrived at Grand-Dessus, which was a kind of platform jutting out like a peak from the ridge. In good weather, the view extends from there for more than 100 kilometers on both sides. Nothing could be seen, but Métrailler was not looking to see anything in terms of a view. He held his gaze now toward the sky. He sat down on the frozen snow and lifted his head with astonishment toward a window that had just appeared a little above him and to the south through the thinning canopy of fog, on the other side of a great ridge of mountain that we began to be able to see. It was there, indeed, where it came out—the sun—or something that could have been the sun, and it was there that it must have come out from behind the mountain, just in time to hide itself again.

But it had grown red and the rock where Métrailler was standing became red; and the sun up above had not shown itself, although it seemed that we had shown it; it had not risen, although it seemed that we had lifted it: disheveled, and all wrapped up, entwined with clouds which were themselves like clots of blood.

Exactly like a severed head around which the beard and hair still hung smoking; that we lifted in the air a moment, only to let fall again. And already the fog and the darkness had come back to their place.

Then, around four o'clock Old Man Métrailler went out of his house. "Is it daytime yet? Hey, everyone, tell me, where could Cyprien have gotten to?"

"Hey, everyone, all of you who can see... because he went out this morning. And now I'm going outside because we've got to find him, only I can't see anything..."

He tapped the ground around him with his cane.

"He didn't make a sound," he was saying, "he left on his bare feet from the house. And now where has he gotten to?"

He was saying, "Hey, everyone."

Because he was still alone on the street, but we were coming because he was speaking loudly; we were coming, we were speaking to him, and he was saying, "You, who are you?" and it was Follonnier who said, "Placide Follonier." And then Lamon who said, "Erasme Lamon." And then more people, men, women, and even Old Brigitte.

Follonnier started speaking, "Don't worry, he's sure to come back. You know his legs must have been itching, having had to stay still so long. Keeping still isn't easy for boys like him. He must have set off up the mountain, toward the goats, with Tissières."

But then someone said, "He isn't with Tissières."

"How do you know?"

"You just have to go and ask him, Tissières I mean, he hasn't left his house."

"Then you must go get him quickly, my boy," said Old Man Métrailler. "Oh, I don't see you, I see you all so pale, you're just like the shadows of yourselves, or maybe the daylight is just bad…"

"The daylight isn't so good, and it's already nighttime; you know it comes early, and the sky is all cloudy."

But he was looking all around with his faded red-rimmed eyes, his eyes which were like the eggshell from a quail—gray with a hint of blue.

Now Tissières had arrived and was saying, "I didn't want to go with him and I told him it wasn't safe but he didn't want to listen…"

Tears started to run from Old Man Métrailler's eyes, even if he held them wide open, and he wasn't moving his eyelids as the water slowly leaked, like the sap of a tree.

Then he leaned abruptly forward, making holes in the snow with his cane and we ran after him; we were saying, "Where are you going?"

He said, "I'm going to find him." We held him back by the arm, he fought us. "Are you going to let him die all alone?"

"We can't go after him, the night is coming. And besides, where do you want to go?"

"Well, light some fires."

"There's fog."

"Well, we've got to ring the bell, or shoot some rifles; he'll move toward the sound. Tissières, go get your rifle."

The village was turned upside down because Tissières went to get his military rifle and his blank cartridges. He shot into the air.

Every once in a while he shot again, holding his weapon toward the sky which was so low it seemed like Tissières was going to touch it with the tip of his rifle.

Meanwhile the houses emptied one by one, women and children spilling out onto the flagstones and into the small streets, asking, "What's going on?"

"Métrailler's gotten lost."

It was nearly evening; lamps were lit in the kitchens, and as the men had returned they held their storm lamps in their hands— lamps with handles like a basket; like the ones used in hay-filled stables or in barns filled with silage; which is why the flame must be protected. Which is why it's surrounded by a thick glass globe, which is then itself surrounded by an iron armature protecting it from shocks.

The lamps made small red dots that hovered a little above the ground, quivering like drops of fine rain.

And those who carried them said, "What's happening?" while Tissières shot off another round; after which everyone was silent, to listen if there wasn't going to be a response; somewhere, on the mountain, beyond the wall of fog, and on top of which the night was coming to cover it like a second wall.

A shot from the rifle, and they listen; a shot to your left; they listen again, a little while later there is a second shot to your right, then three or four shots in succession, but quiet ones, muted, slow ones which barely reach you, and which finish in a kind of long sigh—that's all.

So we saw Old Man Métrailler getting agitated again; and he went forward with his cane, saying, "I'm going anyway, even if you're not coming with me."

There was nothing to do but follow him.

They tilted their storm lanterns to try to read in the snow the places where he had walked, writing small letters here and there in the snow to make words, words that made sentences like on a telegram; they walked around in a kind of chaos, not knowing much what they were going to do, when they suddenly heard the sound of the horn behind them.

It was Jean Antide coming; he was blowing on his copper horn, the one tipped with an antler.

It's a shepherd's horn, and it must be heard far and wide when the shepherd heads out in the early morning, stopping from house to house and gathering his animals one by one; it must be heard far and wide in the evening, too, when he's coming back, so that the women can come and pick up their animals without making him wait.

Jean Antide, Isabelle's brother-in-law, had been a goat shepherd; so he blows into his horn and laughs.

We saw the flash of his teeth—how they shone in the night because of his dark face; and he had curly hair.

"Listen, if you want I'll go ahead and I'll blow my horn. Because Métrailler, he knows the sound well, and so if he's lost… I'll blow from time to time, that should work, and I can even blow two notes when I want."

He blew two notes by changing the position of his tongue; we held up the storm lanterns to see better, and the copper of his horn shone in their light.

"And the horn carries farther than your rifle shots, Tissières, and it's easier to hear where the sound is coming from; it's longer, it's softer; yours is jumping around all over the mountain, you're everywhere and nowhere. Do you want me to?"

We had caught up with Old Man Métrailler, we took him by the arm. Jean Antide went in front; there were about a dozen men. The women were saying, "My goodness, my goodness!" They had made the children go back inside, then, coming back out themselves and having closed the doors behind them, they were watching into the distance at these little fire lights moving away, these pink droplets, which had grown pale, and while growing pale spread out like ink on blotting paper and little by little dissipated, even if they should have, in normal weather, continued to be visible for a long time because of the steep slope of the village they were slowly climbing.

It's this weather. It isn't just that it's nighttime; it's that the air is no longer air. The air is sooty like ashes, opaque like sand.

Jean Antide blew one note, and sometimes he blew two notes. We were holding Old Man Métrailler by the arm.

There was still no wind, which meant that this morning's footprints were hardly erased. They told each other they had to follow them as long as they could, because he'll surely follow them coming back, even if they were mostly thinking that something bad had happened to him, because otherwise he would've already come back.

And Old Man Métrailler said to them, "Are you sure we're on his footprints?"

"By God," we said.

Because of the deep cold and the lack of wind, we saw their breath steaming from their mouths when they leaned over their lanterns; and leaning over their lanterns, they only had to hold them a little to the side to make the footprints even more visible because the print filled with shadow; which is why they said, "There's no way to miss them."

But Métrailler said to Jean Antide, "Blow your horn." A short moment would pass and he said to Jean Antide, "Blow two notes."

And so Cyprien was called like the thrush is called by a duck whistle, but it was a duck whistle that carried a great distance, much farther than a man's voice—the group of them stopped, listened, then started again, all of them making a noise in the snow like breaking glass, then there was a sound like the *hunh!* the logger makes when he settles his axe into the trunk of a tree.

In this way they walked for a good half hour; they were beginning to get discouraged. So much so that if Old Man Métrailler hadn't been there pushing them to keep going, telling Jean Antide all the time to blow and then again blow, and Antide blew, they would surely have ended up going back the way they came. But Antide kept blowing; and this is how they arrived up at the ridge, hesitant to start walking on it, when Antide blew one more time.

And all of them, stopped up there so high, they held their breath; they had to wait for their hearts to stop beating and it took them some time because of how hard they beat, like kicks against a door, and which only slowly quieted.

They listened, but there was nothing.

They listened again, there was still nothing but this sound inside of you which grows quiet as it settles, leaving in its wake the immense silence that covers the land as if the world no longer existed; that feels like we were no longer on earth, like we were suspended high above the earth in the great desert of silently spinning stars.

They listen, there was nothing, still nothing; but suddenly it was Old Man Métrailler who raised his arm up to his ear and cupped his hand around the fold of his ear. "It's him, it's him! Don't you hear?"

We didn't dare contradict him; we didn't dare say a thing.

And everyone was quiet once more, then we didn't know if it was from joy or because he was crying, and maybe he was crying with joy, but there were tears in the old man's voice.

"Listen! Listen, he's calling, it's coming closer."

"From where?"

"There, down below. Where are we?"

"We're up high, we're on the ridge."

"Well, he's down there, below, to the right... don't you hear it?"

"Ah," he said, "it's because you see, and we're never given everything at the same time; you all have eyes, but I have my ears."

So we told him to be quiet.

He went quiet; and the rest of them, one after the other, had begun to hear the cries that were coming from below and from all the way at the bottom of the gorge; weak, uncertain cries that were so exhausted on their way up they were weightless and feeble in the air.

"Blow! Blow two notes!"

Jean Antide blew into his horn.

"Blow again, and blow harder, so he'll know for sure we're here."

Now the cries became more distinct, because we must have gotten closer, we had moved closer to them, we had to find a way to meet them.

44

But what were they going to have to do? Tissières said, "We'll have to go and get him. I'll do it, Antide will come with me. Give me a lantern, and Antide, you take the other lantern."

We asked him if it was safe.

"Let me do it," he said. "This terrain... it knows me."

They had made Old Man Métrailler sit down in the snow, watching the lantern lights widen as they went down. They quickly widened as they weakened and then they vanished; but there was the sound of the horn and there was this voice that answered; and the sound of the horn and the voice finally must have met each other, because now we couldn't hear the voice or the horn...

They had to carry Cyprien, or nearly, to bring him back to the village. They kept their lights on the space where young Métrailler had to place his feet, because he could hardly keep himself upright. He staggered like someone who was drunk. His face was white; his torn hood hung around his neck. His carbine was gone, his hat was gone. He said nothing. He answered our questions with gestures and only barely; so much so that Tissières and Antide wound their arms around his waist and he threw his own around their necks.

Fortunately, we just had to walk down; fortunately, the snow was hard.

And his father kept saying, "How is he? Is he hurt?"

"Of course he's not."

"So why isn't he speaking?"

"He's tired."

And Old Man Métrailler said, "Cyprien, are you really there? Is it true you aren't hurt? Why isn't he answering? Let me touch him."

FIVE

All this time we were watching Brigitte go every morning to pick up dead wood from a thicket of larch that was a little above the village. By wearing shoes that were much too big for her she opened up a little path in the snow; and because each day she made several trips, the path remained, just like a bit of basting thread one has forgotten on a household sheet.

And so it was easy to go from her house into the wood; but things became complicated when she reached the larch trees, because the dead branches were stuck in the frozen snow, from which usually only their tips were sticking out; which meant she had to dig around them with her hands.

We had started just by teasing her, "What are you doing? You don't have enough wood?"

"Of course I have enough."

"Then what?"

"It's in case the sun doesn't return."

She was standing there, hunched over beneath the weight of her sticks, her black skirt rubbed with a kind of gray dust, her face completely yellowed with its coffee-colored spots against the background of the white slope:

"And," she continued, "Of course, like always, I have my provisions to last me until spring, but if there isn't any spring, if instead of getting brighter just then the nighttime comes, if instead of heat comes an increasing cold... you've got to take precautions."

And the women began to be worried, "Well now, look here, is this true?"

"Look here," they said, "Are things like that possible?"

"He said because the earth is in the air, it can simply start to tilt to one side."

"In the air?"

"Yes, in the air, it isn't held up by anything, a ball that turns in the air and isn't fixed; and if none of us can see it move it's only because we're moving with it... so, you understand, nothing but a little tap..."

"How do you know this?"

"Anzévui told me," she said. "Wait for me to go put down my sticks..."

She went into her house, then came back, because she liked to talk; there was still the same low sky, immobile and dark, beneath which now many women were standing around her.

"He hardly speaks anymore," said Brigitte, "but once in a while he will. He turns the pages of his book; that makes a sound. He sits beneath his plants in front of the fire."

"Oh," she continued, "It's just that he isn't doing very well, he's getting weaker and weaker every day. He can hardly move himself around. He goes from his bed to his chair and from his chair to his bed. He told me he won't last longer than the sun. He told me that when the sun goes out, he'll go out... he said, 'you'll find me dead downstairs and you'll look for the sun in the sky but it won't be moving any more than I will.' And I asked him when this would be, and he told me to wait, you see he's always starting again with his calculations, with a little bit of pencil on a little scrap of paper... he says this is what's hard, he told me it would be about fifteen weeks yet; so every Sunday I put a nail in the wall and I've already put seven... and then," she said, "I've lit my oil lamp, because I still have a jug of rapeseed oil in case the night comes suddenly—at least I'll have my light."

She had done what she'd said. Each night we saw the light in her kitchen window, and the window stayed lit all night long, and even when the daylight came the light stayed lit. All day long this light kept shining against the dark wood façade, where we could see it, because the day was so dark, and meanwhile Brigitte pulled a stool out for herself.

It's that she's very small, but luckily the ceiling was low. She went to get an axe, she went to take a cardboard box on which was written: *nails 6 cm*. She climbed up on her stool, she raised her arm, and tilting the top of her body backwards, she hammered the shiny nail into the side of the beam crusted with smoke where there were already seven.

She counted; now there were eight.

I add a nail each Sunday.

Then she went to see if there was still oil in the lamp; the wick rested there with its small flame at the tip; and the wick hangs toward the bottom, but the flame towards the sky.

Because it's a *crésus*, as we call them; a flat round pewter bowl, with a lip and a half-circle handle by which it can also be hung on an iron wire.

She filled the oil lamp: she trimmed the wick without putting it out, and in this way we'll have light when the great light will go out.

It was Sunday morning. What do we see here in the winter? We see nothing. The daylight was something gray and vague that twisted itself slowly beyond the night on the other side of the clouds like something behind a frosted glass.

What do we hear? Nothing at all. Not even the sound of footsteps because of the snow, not even the sound of the wind, because there is never any wind. From time to time a voice, sometimes a child crying, never a bird, not even the fountain, because the fountain runs in a wooden tree trunk to keep it from icing over—which is what would happen if we let it flow freely in the air.

The bells don't even ring out here, because there isn't even a church.

Everyone must go down for services to the church in Lower Saint-Martin, which means they have for a good half-hour walk.

And so on Sunday mornings we get ready to walk down—meaning that the men shave at the crosshatched window onto which they hang a little round mirror in a metal frame or a small square mirror with a dark wood frame; some of them shave with a straight razor, the young men use safety razors which are drawn down the cheek like a hand plane across a piece of wood; but neither the old ones nor the young ones could see anything that morning and as they cut themselves, they cried out, "Son of a ...!"

The road had only been opened up with the little triangle so that it was much narrower than in summer, not much more than a meter wide; it was just a surface path, not having been cleared down to the pavement. We walk forward between two knee-high walls and upon a thick layer of pressed snow. First came three old women, because they go slowly and are careful. Three old women, all in black, all small and hunched over, because we get smaller as we get older. Leaning forward, their hands clasped, their heads in black kerchiefs, a thick woolen shawl wrapped around their chests and tied at the back; they were not speaking. Sometimes we can hear the bells from Lower Saint-Martin all the way up here, because they have four of them and a good bell ringer who knows how to get them going and has experience with all kinds of bells; but today we couldn't hear them, either because the air was so still or because of the snow which is like a cotton covering and mutes out the sound; it was a Sunday without bells. And now in the low light there were more women coming, and then the girls. This is when we heard Isabelle's laughter. Ah! At least she was laughing, at least she was shining; this young woman, you can see her from afar, with her sky blue silk bodice and her apron with its thin stripes in all different colors, her pink scarf at her neck.

She was with two friends, and because the path was not wide enough to pass with three at the same time, her two friends went a little bit in front, one on each side, and she was a bit behind and in the middle.

We see them turn around, they ask her a question.

She looked all around her, as if checking to be sure that no one was going to hear her.

"Of course, it's Augustin."

"Another one!"

"Why not?"

The two others were astonished.

"Only," Isabelle said, "you have to know how to manage it."

And then her laugh rang out like the earliest blackbird singing his bright notes in the morning silence.

"Oh, you have to know how to do it. He said to me, 'You already have two dresses.' I told him, 'Two, what does that mean? Don't you want your wife to be well-dressed sometimes? Let's go to Anthamatten then.' Augustin just sold a calf; you have to take advantage of the occasion. I told him, 'It'll only take three meters, that's all, at five francs the meter. And you know that Anthamatten has the best fabrics; they're solid, they last, they're worth the price.' He didn't want to. But then a girl puts a hand on their shoulder, or maybe takes them by the arm; they have to feel your warmth through their jacket or a little lower. A girl says, 'Shall we go inside and look?' And, when they eventually want to, well, you see, that's when we don't want to anymore..."

And laughing, she continued, "Then a girl says, 'Maybe it's too expensive; let's go then, we'd better go now.' But by now they're the one who wants to, they're forcing you to, 'None of that, since we're here!' They're the one who chooses the best fabric; we just have to let them do it and then praise them, tell them, 'You'll see, you'll see, all the other women will be jealous!' They're happy."

She was laughing. "And it's just... it's just that when the weather is horrible we must make ourselves beautiful, when the weather is sad we must be happy; don't you think so? In the depths of winter is when we must turn ourselves toward spring."

Only, what if the spring never came, never again? This is what the older women were discussing as they walked down. But they told themselves not to speak to anyone else about it, not to those down in the lower village, they said, "They'll just make fun of us." And then the men were coming and going in groups, five or six together, dressed in brown or in black, with fur caps or felt hats, hands in their pockets; and there was Old Man Métrailler being led by the arm by his son. There was Revaz with his knee, though his knee was doing better. He said, "It's getting better, there's nothing to say about it... it's Anzévui." He was walking beside Pralong; he was saying, "It's his compresses... the swelling has gone, my leg is still just a little stiff, but Anzévui told me to work it out. And you see, my cane; well, I've taken it in case I need it, but for the moment..." He put it beneath his arm. "You see?"

"You know," he continued, "That Anzévui is actually quite smart: he's a wise man. He doesn't just understand things, but how things work. You see that I was right to listen to him."

"You saw him again?" asked Pralong.

"Of course, I went to show him my leg. I had to, you know he doesn't leave the house. He isn't doing very well; he's there beneath his plants, doing his calculations. You know, if he wasn't wrong about my knee, maybe he isn't wrong about what's going on with... what do you think?"

"It's still for April 13th?"

"That's what he says. But it's best to keep this between us..."

"And to be ready for it."

"If you think so."

"To put one's affairs in order..."

They passed along, they disappeared; and now it was Follonier coming along with Arlettaz.

He'd let his beard grow out. He hadn't shaved for three weeks now. The hairs had grown perfectly straight, black and white, from all sides, all around his face, and they mixed in with his hair that he hadn't cut either, so that it was like he had two heads, a bearded one, enormous and round, and in the middle a head with skin, also round, with two small blue eyes.

"But you remember her, don't you, Follonier? It hasn't been so long since she left. How long has it been now?" He counted in his head, then, "It'll be three years this spring... and well, what do you say about it, Follonier, wasn't she just beautiful?"

"Oh, of course," said Follonier.

They were the last to come down the path and were much farther behind the others, but they didn't seem to be in a hurry because Arlettaz kept stopping here and there.

"I'm not shaving anymore, what's the use of it? It's just that she was beautiful, you see..."

The path winds. The path is narrow and white. The path feels like we have a carpet beneath our feet, because of the soft, strong snow: only this thickness of snow that the little triangle had left between us and the pavement. The snow makes a little wall on the side of the mountain, another little wall on the side of the valley; we don't have to pay attention to which direction we're going because the path is made, and we're kept on our way by these walls.

But suddenly Follonier stopped, interrupting Arlettaz, "You see?"

He held his arm so low that he seemed to be showing the top of his shoe; but he was pointing at the ravine over the little snow wall. There was nothing to do but let the eye roll down like a stone for two hundred meters: "There, next to the pine tree, do you see it? It's square, it's gray, it looks like a big stone. You know what that is? The doctor's car, the one who drove himself off the road last year."

Arlettaz only nodded his head; Arlettaz continued, "Like on a coin. You remember at the café, when they were teasing me, 'Come on, Arlettaz, you're making money off your daughter; this looks like her; how much does the government give you?' They got out a coin from their pockets, you remember that? I didn't say anything, of course, but I was thinking they were right, it does look like her.

"Well," he continued, "Nineteen years old, and with a face on a coin; beautiful and well-built and tall; she gets it from her mother and from me, but her mother is dead; and didn't I deserve to keep her? Say, how about that, I just couldn't."

Follonier shrugged his shoulders; Follonier said, "We never can."

The road turned once again, and the view in ordinary weather changes at the same time, completely, because sometimes we're walking north and sometimes east, sometimes west. Sometimes we go in the direction of the mountains which climb high on the other side of the gorge, 2000 meters above you, sometimes we go along the side of the lowlands which are 1000 meters lower and we glide along above them like in an airplane. That day we saw nothing but a little bit of the path in front of us, a bit of hillside to one side, emptiness to the other.

"Do you understand anything about it?"

"No one understands anything about anything."

"Why did she leave?"

"Why would she have stayed?"

"Because," Arlettaz was saying, "Because... you've got to admit, Follonier, that she was my daughter... and what good is a daughter if she's not there? A daughter makes a man happy, and when she's far away, so is his happiness."

"You should have told her that."

"I didn't dare."

He thought, then he started again, "And, well, a man doesn't know..."

Some ravens, which they couldn't see, cried out from time to time in the sky above them. From time to time, from amongst the pine trees standing along the steep hillside, some jays, which they couldn't see either, made noises like a rusty weathervane in gusts of wind. And Arlettaz was thinking that this is what happened, that he didn't know how. He wondered then if he had known how. We watched Arlettaz shake his head, walking with his arms apart, his hat in his hand; but there was no response for him but the cries of the ravens and the laughter of the jays.

"This one here," said Follonier, "that's Antonelli's truck."

This time there was a little rock wall sitting atop another small wall of stones, with a flat space between them, and there, on the flat space, was the overturned truck, its wheels in the air, but there were only two left.

"And," Arlettaz said, "what should I do? And you know I've looked for her. Two years I've been looking for her... and you have to understand, if people are saying it's the end of the world, well, I can only say that it's for the best. Because then I won't need to look for her anymore. All over the country, from the headwaters of the Rhône to the lake, it'll be three years soon, I can finally have a rest. And it's coming at the right time, because I've got nothing left."

But this was surely where Follonier was waiting for him, "Nothing at all?"

"No, nothing," said Arlettaz. "All this traveling is expensive, and it makes a man thirsty, what can I say? I sold my goats, I sold my cows, I sold my pastures, nothing left but my tools. Do you want to buy my tools?"

"No," said Follonier, "I've got all the tools I need. But what about your field in Empeyres?"

"It's not for sale."

"What good is it to you, if this is the end?"

"And for you?"

"Who says I'm willing to go?"

"It's just that it's a good field; it's the best place around for growing rye. Really, Follonier, would you like this field?"

"Oh!" Follonier answered, "I'm not so bothered about it... only, I see exactly what you need. You're right, you want to be free. And you're thinking that if this is really the end, it wouldn't be so bad to have a little money in your pocket as you wait it out. If I buy the field from you, it's just to do you a favor..."

The road crossed through a stand of larch that had lost their little green feathers, but the snow had taken their place with its soft quilt. The wood was gray and white instead of green and gray. It was like a patchy cloud of smoke and through the patches we couldn't tell whether we were looking at snow laden branches or the hillside that was behind them. Then Lower Saint-Martin appeared; the village

sits in a hollow and has many houses with low roofs all closely settled around a large stone church.

"How much?"

"Well, I don't know."

They walked a few steps more without saying anything, then Follonier said, "Around five hundred."

"Fifteen hundred," said Arlettaz.

The church bells had finished ringing for a while now. We heard
that they had started to sing beneath the nave; the door stays open
for those who do not go inside, those who listen to mass from outside at the door, taking their hats off from time to time.

"Listen," said Follonier, "You want to talk about this again to-
night at Pralong's? Bring a paper in case we might come to an understanding."

They attended the service, they walked back up to Upper
Saint-Martin; there was a short day of six or seven hours, that was
all, because of the sky being so unwell and the height of the mountains; after which we had seen a drop of fire tremble in the dusky
shadow.

That's how the day finished. Another day. And how many more
would there be? How many more weeks would there be?

"And how much do you spend each week?"

Pralong didn't seem to be listening. Pralong was reading the newspaper. Fat Sidonie was trying to adjust the wireless. But Follonier
wouldn't let Arlettaz alone, knowing not to let a deal go until it was
brought to its right conclusion. He'd made Arlettaz sit in front of
him.

He's a good talker, he was saying to Arlettaz, "Come on, how
much do you need per day?"

He had his pipe in the corner of his mouth, and there was a kind of smile on the other side of his mouth; but his eyes were not moving as he stared fixedly at Arlettaz, "How much do you need per day? And how much do you drink per day? Oh, you can overestimate... so, ok, let's say five liters. And then you've also got to go to the barber. Food, wine, taxes, but never mind taxes, taxes don't matter if everything is ending in April... it doesn't matter, let's put it all together."

"There's also travel, that's what costs the most."

"What travel?"

"Well," said Arlettaz, "Just now I have to go all the way to Le Bouveret; it's the only part of the canton I haven't tried yet; and who knows, it's on the water, maybe she likes the water."

"You told me that it wasn't worth looking anymore."

"I'd prefer she be with me when the end comes, because then we'll pass over together."

"Fine, add the travel."

"I've already been to Brig, I've already been to the Germans and, on the other side, I went to Martigny, to Saint-Maurice, Monthey; all that's left is the lake shores where the fish huddle in groups, the little ones in the shallows, the big ones in the deeps."

"750?"

"No."

"800?"

"No."

The young men were coming in. There were six of them, including Lucien Revaz; he said, "Evening, Sidonie."

"And here I was thinking you'd put all that behind you."

But they were twirling Sidonie by the waist, because there were several of them and being several makes them more enterprising. They were gay; they weren't listening to what the men were talking about. They went to sit at the other end of the room, three on a bench, three on another bench. "Hands off of me, or else!" said Sidonie, holding her hand up, and the young men were laughing.

"Well, then bring us something to drink," they said to her.

They set themselves down, they brought their faces closer together as they rested their elbows on the brown painted tables and leaned in, and all around them was the wood paneling that rose halfway up the walls. They got the wireless to work, a waltz was playing; then came news of the war in Spain; so they were all quiet together, they listened, and then a long moment of silence.

This is when we could hear Arlettaz saying, "I have put it behind me..."

"It doesn't seem like it," answered Follonnier.

The young men pushed each other with their elbows.

They leaned again toward each other: "It's all Anzévui's fault; they've all lost their minds."

They turned toward Arlettaz. They saw that the straight hairs of his beard were sticking out a good two centimeters all around his face, just above his shirt with its ripped collar and beneath a fur cap which seemed like it was a continuation of his beard; and in the middle was the round of his face, and in the round of his face there were two little blue eyes. They were thinking that this was all he needed, he'd already gone crazy because of his daughter; now he'd gone crazy two times over.

They pushed each other with their elbows, they spoke in low voices.

Then Lucien said suddenly, "It isn't just him...there's also my father."

He called Sidonie, "You know about it. Say, have you seen Gabrielle today? I couldn't go to meet her. My father's forbidding it... he's also, he's lost his mind, because I was thinking to get married at the end of the winter; and well, my father doesn't want me to. She doesn't dare come to see me; I don't dare go to see her... And we don't have any money, neither her nor me."

He said, "Sidonie sends messages for us... you're a good girl, Sidonie."

He said, "There's my brother in the vineyards: and I think I'm going to join him because at least he's got the lake to distract him, he's got water, all that blue, and two suns is what he said; and we've got nothing but white..."

"White!" said one of the young men, "It's more like gray."

"Yes, gray and hardly any sun."

"And even less in a little while..."

But with this they burst out laughing; and at the other table, Follonnier said, "900."

Arlettaz and Follonnier said nothing more at all, and they were not looking at each other either, even though they were sitting face to face; all they did was lift their glasses from time to time and say, "Cheers!"

Arlettaz was thirsty and so Sidonie brought a liter. Follonnier mentioned a number, Arlettaz shook his head. And that was all.

But now all the noise was coming from the other side of the room, because they're young and the young are noisy.

They were saying to Sidonie, "So you'll come with us? Because we need you, that Anzévui deserves some trouble, you see. So we need a girl... you'll tell him something's wrong, something's wrong, you need some fennel tea..."

They were staring at her bulging stomach beneath her apron, because she was a large person.

"And who knows, maybe you won't have to tell him a lie."

"Scoundrels! Let go of me!"

"Who knows; you'll tell him it's the end of the month; you'll ask if you can come in, and meanwhile we'll hide."

But she ran away into the kitchen and we heard her close the door with the lock.

"A thousand!"

Follonier had shouted the word but the young men at the back table hadn't heard it: they were laughing too much and too heartily. Arlettaz's fur cap got the word because he was holding his head down; the word got that fur cap to rise up, bringing with it a little round face that was in the middle of his beard like the moon in a halo. And this time he didn't shake it, he didn't say no, he said nothing: he just watched Follonier with his little blue eyes.

"You know it's just because it's you," Follonier said, "and because I want to make sure you end your life well; it's more than half what the field is worth..."

He continued, "But okay, if you're happy with it. Do you have the paper?"

Arlettaz still wasn't speaking.

"I was thinking you wouldn't have one, which is why I prepared one."

He pulled a tatty old brown leather wallet from the lower pocket of his vest. It was tied with string; he had a difficult time untying the string with his fat fingers, taking more time maybe than was necessary, but it was a way to keep hidden the contented smile he couldn't keep from crossing his face; he took a folded piece of paper from the wallet and held it out to Arlettaz, who kept still and silent.

"Here."

Written on the paper was this: *The undersigned agrees to sell the following item to Mr. Placide Follonier —field in Empeyres, for the sum of* (there was a blank space). And below this, the word *Signature*.

"This is just until we can go to the notary, because we'll have to make an appointment first. Sign it if you agree."

"How much will you advance me, in cash?" Arlettaz said. "I've got nothing."

"How much do you want?"

"A hundred francs."

"Fifty."

But this time Arlettaz kept firm. He wanted his hundred francs and right away. Follonier sighed. And then, "We need a pen and some ink; we'll add this to the paper: *one hundred francs received*, and you sign. Hey, Sidonie!"

He saw that she was no longer there, he saw that the door to the kitchen was closed. The young men in the corner had begun to speak in low voices; and every once and awhile, one or another of them threw a glance over their shoulders at the two men. Follonier got up. Follonier tried to open the door to the kitchen, it was locked.

"Say, Sidonie, where are you?... I need something to write with."

She opened the door a crack but held the bottom of it with her foot.

"What's the matter?" asked Follonier. "What's gotten into you? I need a pen and some ink..."

"Where," he asked, "where do you mean?"

Because she was refusing to let him go in. "Behind the box for the wireless."

She closed the door again; he went to look behind the wireless; he saw that it was not working, someone must have turned the button, then he went back to sit down; and meanwhile the boys were saying, "So it's understood, we'll go. You'll be the girl, Lucien. Only Sidonie doesn't want to lend us her clothes."

"But she's got to, if she wants us to pay her."

"An old skirt, a bodice, a kerchief and then whatever you need to make a nice white face for you, Lucien; and then use a matchstick for your eyebrows, that's all... and something to make you a bit round in the front."

"Just roll your vest up into a ball."

While he took his vest off, they all kept watching over to the other table to be sure they hadn't been heard; in this way they saw Arlettaz taking the pen and then Arlettaz must have written something, then Follonnier had held out his hand like he was waiting for the paper to be passed to him, but Arlettaz didn't agree: so Follonnier had opened his wallet.

Arlettaz started to tap the table with his empty liter; luckily it was made from a heavy glass with a thick bottom, because no one was coming and Arlettaz was tapping it harder and harder.

Finally, the door to the kitchen opened: "What is it?"

And Arlettaz said, "A liter. I've got money."

Follonnier got up and said, "I'm off to bed then."

Eventually Sidonie ended up having to come over, because her job required it, and having slipped through the door that she had only half-opened, she came just to Arlettaz's table with his liter.

"Say!" they were saying, "Hey, Sidonie, listen, we promise, we'll leave you alone, we have something to ask you."

"Come on, Sidonie, you don't believe us, well, look…"

And Lucien and the others, with the index finger of their right hands placed over the index of their left, they made the sign of the cross.

Arlettaz had filled his glass, had emptied it immediately, had filled it again.

"What do you want now?" Sidonie said.

She spoke to them from over the threshold of the kitchen, all mistrustful, ready to close the door on herself if she needed to; and they were laughing quietly, they motioned with their shoulders to Arlettaz at his table, his head leaning over his crossed arms; but he seemed to see nothing and seemed to hear nothing, occupied as he was with the things inside of him, his eyes turned inward.

"Are you coming?"

She took a step toward them, they gestured her to come nearer.

"Listen…"

She saw that she could go all the way over.

"Listen, don't you have an old skirt and an old bodice to lend us?"

"What for?"

They were speaking quietly. They indicated toward Arlettaz.

"We'll tell you that another time."

"And then a little flour and some water…"

"And then a mirror…"

And they said, "What if we went into the kitchen…"

Sidonie was curious; at the same time she saw that the boys were caught up in their idea and weren't thinking about her so her curiosity won out. "If you want."

They passed in front of Arlettaz; Arlettaz didn't move. We couldn't tell if what we could see was his fur cap or the top of his head. We couldn't tell if what we could see was his beard or his hair. They were all thinking that he was getting drunk, like he did sometimes.

And, having gone into the kitchen, having pushed the door behind them: "You see, Sidonie, because you don't want to come along, it's Revaz who will be the girl. Yes, stand there so he can copy you...We just need a pillow now, if you've got one; we'll bring it back to you. We're going to dress as a girl and visit Anzévui, but girls have white skin, and girls are rounder, so you've got to help us..."

"Sidonie," they were saying, "you've got to give us a kiss."

But this time she laughed, then she left the room while they went hunting around in the cupboard where they found flour and put some in a glass.

Sidonie came back with clothes in her arms. She had a skirt and a bodice.

She said, "Oh, you're such imps. And so you're going?" she asked. "And what will you do?"

"It's to scare him, you know... doesn't he deserve it?"

"How are you going to scare him?"

"Well, you know, Revaz will go as a girl. Anzévui must be used to visitors coming at night. He'll say, 'That's five francs.' We'll give him five francs, then we can go in... you'll just have to be careful, Lucien, that he doesn't recognize you..."

Meanwhile Revaz was putting the skirt on, and then Sidonie arranged his chest since she knew how to do it.

"And be careful what you're going to say to him, and be careful about your voice. Try first, because we're here, and we'll tell you if it's okay."

"Eh, Mr. Anzévui, my dear Mr. Anzévui, I'm not so well."

Revaz had a little girl's voice. We told him it was good.

"I don't know; it didn't come last month; that will be fifteen days now. So I've come to you to see if you might have something for me... anything, Mr. Anzévui?"

"It's good."

They burst out laughing, then stood in front of Lucien Revaz with the glass of flour, and with the corner of a wet towel they whitened his face.

"Because you need to look sickly, of course, and it'll also hide your beard... Now, put your kerchief. Move it a bit forward on your forehead... do you have a match? Good, light it."

And with the charcoal from the match, they put some black around his eyes.

"You still need some lipstick, like girls from town. Don't you have some, Sidonie? Too bad... hey, how about some syrup?"

Because there were plenty of half-full syrup bottles on a shelf next to the door; and they uncorked a bottle of raspberry syrup and by wetting the other corner of the towel they passed it over his lips. They held out a mirror:

"What do you think?"

"Jiminy!" Lucien didn't think he was ugly, he even thought he was pretty. He began to laugh to show them his teeth which had become whiter because of the lipstick...

"Well, that's it. So do we go?"

"Let's go. And you understand, Sidonie, the rest of us will be the police. Because we'll let Revaz go in and then we'll bang on the door, "'Open up! In the name of the law! No need to explain, we heard everything...Open up!'"

They were speaking quietly now, and Sidonie said, "Be careful. Arlettaz is here. He could tell on you..."

But one of them had cracked the door open, slipping a head through the opening, and looked to see what Arlettaz was doing; Arlettaz hadn't moved, only his liter was empty.

They told Sidonie to go refill his drink... are you ready, they asked each other... because, you know, we'll bring Anzévui; we'll tell him we're going to lock him up; and there'll be a ditch somewhere with just enough powdery snow to send him for a swim.

They didn't need to pass through the café: the kitchen had a second door that opened up to the outside. It was maybe about eleven o'clock in the evening. There wasn't a single star. Luckily one of the boys took an electric flashlight from his pocket. These boys are modern. They like new things. We only had to press a button.

They went forward along the little street; and so they saw these two drops of fire hanging in a bit of nothing, one nearby and a little below them to the right, the other farther off and vague, above them.

"Look at that, would you!" they said. "It's all that old man's fault..."

Indicating the lower light, they said, "It's Brigitte's oil lamp because she's keeping it lit all the time." And above them was the other window with its light, and they said, "It's the crazy old man, because he spends a part of the night reading in his books; just the thing to bring bad luck on the village, because he must be a bit of a wizard, but we'll show him we're even more of one when we want to be."

Lucien Revaz went forward alone in the direction of the light in the window; the rest of them went to hide, two on one side of the house and three on the other.

They watched Revaz walk up and could see him vaguely enough because of the glimmer that came from the wall and into which he entered—he looked exactly like one of our young girls, a poor girl;

and she clasped her hands over her belt and leaned her head beneath her kerchief, while the boys stifled their laughter.

"Mr. Anzévui... Oh, dear old Mr. Anzévui, open please..." She knocked on the window pane.

The others watched from behind the corner of the house and there was a long moment, and then she started again, "Open please, Mr. Anzévui, I need your help... Oh, I really need your help..."

No one was coming; she knocked again on the window.

"Mr. Anzévui, it's urgent... oh, please, Mr. Anzévui, have pity on me."

But then the boys saw Revaz step back, then step back a bit more; then he turned around abruptly and disappeared into the night.

They raced after him, trying to catch up with him but they didn't dare call out his name; and there was nothing but the light from the flashlight that suddenly turned on, making a white circle on the snow, then it went out just as quickly.

Six

"I hammer a nail; that makes twelve... I hammer a nail every Sunday; I go to see if there's still oil in the lamp, and then I trim the wick."

"I take my axe and get up on a stool, I hold the nail in my left hand and with the back of the axe, I hammer it in."

"The lamp will give light when the sun will be gone. If the sun leaves us completely, I'll still have the lamp."

"Which is why it needs careful watching. I have to make sure the oil doesn't thicken in the bowl; I have to make sure the wick is never too short, never too long; when it's too short it goes out, when it's too long it chars."

She was seated near the window, she was filled with contentment; she didn't know why. Because it was day and the daylight wasn't coming. The day was drawing near, but was the color hanging in the air actually daylight or was it fog? It wasn't real daylight, it was a false light; and it seemed to climb up from the snow to what was above it, as if the feeble light in the thick air came from below, and not from above. But Brigitte was warm behind her window: she had her own light and she could leave it to its business and sit there resting.

"And he says that he doesn't know, that he still doesn't know, but he's calculating. He's beneath his plants, doing his calculations. He sees that the earth is going to tilt and the sun will no longer give light, and so all of us will be in darkness, but what does that matter? If we're ready, if we've got our little lamps, and we'll be seated by our lamp, saying, 'What is fated must fulfill its fate.'"

She was listening; there was nothing to be heard. It had snowed again in the night. There hadn't been any wind, and the snow fell from the sky, it kept falling like a tree losing its leaves. There had never been so many children's noses pressed flat to the windows as there were that morning, because we kept them from going outside. As soon as they woke, they ran to the windows where their breath melted the ice; from outside we saw their faces in a little black round, with a flattened nose and two eyes looking out. Brigitte was keeping very quiet.

"At noon," she thought, "I'll go to Anzévui's. He's also quiet; it's that the two of us have finished our lives." A person goes over their life just before it ends, dreaming of happy moments that were had, which line up like knots in a rope and which keep the rope from slipping too quickly through the hands. This is what she was thinking; meanwhile Isabelle was in bed with her husband Augustin Antide, and above their bed was their policeman cousin in his lovely uniform.

"What time is it?"

"Eight o'clock."

"Already."

There was hardly any light at the small windows; it couldn't be said that the light was coming in. It came toward the window, tapped at the glass and there it was stopped.

"In the summer I'll put flowers in boxes at the window; but what about you, Augustin, what will you do? Why do you need to move already?"

"I'm getting up."

"There's no rush."

"And the animals?"

"You know it's Jean's turn this morning. Oh, you're so restless…"

And then, leaning toward his ear, "What's the matter, Augustin. We're not going to be able to go to mass this morning, there's too much snow. And so for once we can have a nice long lie in, but you can't keep still."

She gently slid her leg against his leg, gently rubbed her thigh against his; then, because he was turning his back to her, she went toward him with the warmth of her chest.

"Oh, you crazy fool," she said. And then she said, "Stop moving!"

And stretching one arm beneath him and the other around him, she went looking for him with her hands.

"Is this because of Anzévui? Well, if the sun... do you know what we'd do? So what if the sun was never coming back? Do you know what the two of us would do? We'd get into bed so we wouldn't be cold."

She blew her warm breath on his neck, little by little bringing him to her, little by little making him turn toward her, "And then do you know what we'd do?"

She went looking for him with her mouth, and pretending in the dark that she was lost, she said, "Augustin, where are you? No, that's not you! That's your prickly chin... and this, what's this? That's your nose, that's not you... but say, do you know what we'd do next? Because there'd be no need to move anymore, or only just a little. Augustin, what if the sun was never coming back? Well, we'd be here, we'd be together... we wouldn't see anything, we wouldn't hear anything, we wouldn't know anything; and it would be just the two of us, because it's lovely when it's just the two of us."

Then there were no more words; just a mouse that came out of its hole in the attic above them, and scampered along; then there

was something that fell, then the sound like someone rolling a walnut;—none of this kept Augustin, an instant later, from jumping
down from the bed and getting quickly dressed.

The next day, or maybe two days later, Cyprien Métrailler was in
his kitchen with Tissières. This was at the beginning of the afternoon; they were in the kitchen, and Old Man Métrailler had gone
upstairs to lie down in his room a moment. There isn't much work
to do in the winter on the mountain, and it's better to sleep than do
nothing. Métrailler had been busy all morning cutting wood and
the old man carried and then stacked it against the wall, which is a
task that doesn't need a pair of eyes because the hands will do the
job. The old man leaned down; we saw him pat the ground around
him; and, picking up the pieces one by one as he met them with his
hand, he stacked them in the crook of his arm like a baby. It was
important to Old Man Métrailler that he showed he was still useful.
And so noon came.

The two young men were now in the kitchen, just below Old
Man Métrailler's room, with a bottle of brandy. Cyprien had placed
the bottle and the two small glasses on a stool between them: and,
from time to time, they were both puffing on their pipes, their feet
warming, having spoken of different things, and now having nothing more to say. Through the window we saw a first roof, then a
second roof, that was all. Both of which, with their two slopes, were
nothing but a sharp triangle of dark wood, but on top of both were
thick white comforters, a half-meter thick. Two enormous bags of
feathers, half-fluffed in a very clean quilt; the only particularity was
the end cut, and on each end cut the different layers were marked
by a darker line, by the differences in the snow's density, by the

differences in its thickness. This is how these white masses came to push back against the gray sky, and it was cold against this gray which was sad.

Suddenly Tissières raised his head; and, without looking at Métrailler, said, "Say..." And then, "You never told me what happened to you."

"When?"

"You know, when we went to find you."

"Oh, I'd have come back on my own..."

Neither man looked at the other one, because Tissières was looking at the fire and smoking his pipe, and Métrailler was looking at his feet, his elbows on his knees, leaning forward.

"Is that true?"

"You saw, I wasn't too far from the village..."

"Yes, but where were you?"

"Well, yes, I was in the ravine..."

"And it was night."

"And so what?" said Métrailler.

The words came with difficulty; he had trouble answering, he was reticent. Only it seemed that Tissières was set on knowing everything and wasn't letting himself be discouraged by his friend's silences. He kept on, "I was worried, you know, because of the ravine, because of the night... and all of us were following your tracks and we had a lantern: you..."

Cyprien sat up, he took his pipe from his mouth. "Don't I know the mountain as well as you do?"

"That's not what I mean. It's just... how did you lose your tracks on the way back?"

They were two friends, they always hunted together; and now

Métrailler abruptly ducked his head again, having seen that it wouldn't be so easy to deceive Tissières. He said, "You're not drinking?"

He filled the empty glasses. They drank, both of them; it was a good warming brandy. It's like a breath of warmth with a perfume that slides down one pipe into the stomach and then climbs up another into your head where it unfreezes your ideas.

So much so that Métrailler decided: "Listen, I climbed all the way to Grand-Dessus."

"To Grand-Dessus!"

"Yes."

"Why do that? And you managed it?"

"I managed it. Why wouldn't I have been able to? And now listen to this. You remember what Anzévui said. Well, it made me eager to see the sun, and I told myself to go looking for it. You didn't want to; so this is all your fault, you know. Don't worry, I'm not mad at you. Forget about it. But God knows that maybe, if you'd been there, we'd have gotten a goat even if we couldn't see twenty steps ahead. Anyway, there'd have been two of us. And you would have seen it as well."

"Seen what?"

"Well," said Métrailler. "You would have seen the severed head, because that's all that I saw."

"The severed head?"

"By God, yes, and all of us are in the fog and maybe we better stay in it until… because it gave me such a shock. I dropped my rifle. I wanted to go and get it, I slipped…"

Just then they heard a crack in the room above them, then almost at the same time a noise like a body falling.

The two men ran to climb up the stairs.

They found Old Man Métrailler stretched out on the floor beside his bed. A bit of foam was coming from his mouth; his eyes were all white.

One of them took him by the shoulders, the other by his feet; he was stiff, although still warm; and they raised him up like he was a statue, a statue carved from gray stone.

There was only a little blood on the floor because he had fallen backward; there was only a little blood in the scoop of the pillow when they laid him down on the bed.

"Are you okay?" Métrailler was saying. "Are you okay? Say something, Father, it's me, can you hear me?"

Meanwhile Tissières had opened the window and was calling out through it, and then he ran outside. And everyone came. And too many people came. The entire village arrived, and people were saying, "What's happened?"— "It's Old Man Métrailler."—"What's happened to him?"—"There's a bit of blood, he fell from his bed." And the women were saying, "Put leaches behind his ears."—"Yes, but where to find any?"—"Make him drink something warm."— "We can't open his mouth."—"Someone call the doctor."

And this was what was finally decided, but the doctor couldn't get on the road until the following morning.

He made half the trip in his car, the other half on a mule that we had sent to meet him. It was Jean Antide, Isabelle's brother-in-law, who led the mule by the bridle. He held it firmly in his closed fist near the bit, because a foot slipped easily in the places where the snow had been built up by the wind, and in other places the ground was frozen beneath the snow that covered it and so the iron-shod hoof could not grip.

We could see them coming around 11:00 am. Old Man Métrailler hadn't moved the entire night: and it was Brigitte who had watched over him with the other women. We could see them coming from far, the doctor and Jean. The mule had no legs; beside the mule was a boy without legs, a shortened person. It was as if the mule's stomach had swollen. It scraped along nearly level with the snowdrifts. Because the mule was like a shovel; and it was as if a team of men had worked in certain places, filling up the holes at the base of the hills. Then, all of a sudden, the beast and the man began to push from the bottom, stretching out, growing taller, had become whole again: it was where the road had been swept, and they appeared in all their height, with the doctor on the mule's back and Jean beside him, with his strangely tanned face, who was speaking and gesticulating: at times showing the village when it could be seen, at times showing through the fog the things that couldn't be seen, things that had been there, the things that weren't there anymore, but which might be there again, some time or another; up high to the right, above and in front of him, where in good weather we could see a white peak, where in good weather we could see black dots moving about in front of a wall of rock: the rock face is pink, it's gray, it shines in the sun like glass; and when evening comes it's like gold. But today we could see nothing. The men coming were seen only by the children who were watching out for them; who began to run to Métrailler's house; who ran crying out, "Here they are! Here they are!"

Old Man Métrailler hadn't moved. Had some curse been brought upon him? Only Brigitte and Cyprien were still in the room.

We went inside; the heavy hobnailed soles made noise on the stairs. We went inside: it was the doctor, a young man; the old man doesn't move. And Cyprien had begun to tell how the accident had happened.

The doctor took Old Man Métrailler's wrist and held up his watch. Old Man Métrailler didn't move. There was a little froth around his lips, like an old neglected mule; his mouth made a steady raspy sound. The doctor shrugged his shoulders. He said, "Do you have any hot water?"

"It's just that he could hardly see at all anymore," Cyprien was saying.

"How old is he?"

"Seventy-five."

"We're going to try to wash his mouth."

He had opened his bag; Brigitte went to get water from the kitchen; he shook several drops of brown liquid into the glass.

"I need a spoon, a tablespoon," he said to Cyprien. "You'll have to help me."

They tried to sit the sick man up in bed, but he resisted unconsciously: his entire body resisted through a kind of self-will and his joints didn't seem to want to work anymore; so much so that they could only lean Old Man Métrailler's body a little by slipping a pillow behind his shoulders.

He still wasn't moving. His half-closed eyes weren't looking at anyone; leaning in a bit, we would have seen that beneath his lids his eyes were as gray as his skin. His eyes weren't looking at anyone, at anything: and the doctor said, "Well then, he isn't suffering, that's already something…" while trying to open his mouth with the handle of the spoon he'd placed between his toothless gums; and saying to Cyprien, "This is just to help his breathing. Hold his head, like that."

But the spoon handle bent, his jaw kept tightly closed; and all the doctor was able to do was moisten a cloth and use it to wipe his lips, and then rolling it around his finger, he wiped the man's palate; but the foam reappeared, and the raspy sound grew louder like a woodworker throwing himself into his work.

"I'm going to try to give him a shot anyway... place an icy cloth on his head; heat some vinegar and apply it to his ankles. We've got to try everything, of course... Just call me tomorrow morning, if he's still here..."

We heard the sound of many people in front of the house, speaking in quiet voices. Because everything was silent now in the bedroom where a little yellow and blue alcohol flame was burning. The entire village took advantage of the doctor's visit, coming to ask for a consultation, as they do; which is why doctors agree to come to the mountains, losing an entire day just traveling, because these places are so far away and the roads so difficult.

The doctor put his syringe away in his case.

"Wait," he said, "you never know... anyway, call me and good luck..."

He shook Cyprien's hand, he went out.

And right away Justine Emonet stopped him. "Oh, Doctor, I don't know what's wrong but my baby isn't well."

Then we saw Revaz approaching, we could tell it was him because of his knee.

The old man upstairs didn't move. He just kept on not moving. He kept on making his steady little noise like a worm in the center of a wooden beam. Night came, people went back to their homes; and then the noise came less regularly, weaker, like a cricket's song when the weather turns foul.

Revaz came in, Revaz went into the room, Revaz took Cyprien to the side and said, "Did you hear? My knee, the doctor saw it... and well, he told me that it was healed. It was a flare up of rheumatism in the joint. And well," Revaz said "you know who healed it? Do you want me to go and get him?"

Cyprien shook his head, "He's bad luck," he said.

"But what are you going to do?"

"I have no idea."

"But you can see your father's going to die, so what does it cost you to try something else?"

"Oh," said Brigitte, who had come closer. "But he's a wise man, he is, he sees deeply... and there's his book, and it's a very old book, and much older than the books these doctors have now... he'll know, he'll know what to do."

Cyprien said nothing else.

So Revaz then went to get Anzévui. And at first Anzévui hadn't wanted to come, but Revaz said to him, "Show them what you know how to do... you already healed my knee and, well, the old man, God knows where he's hurt, but you'll find it, you'll find the problem and hunt it out where it is."

Anzévui said, "It's too far; it's too hard for me to walk."

"The path is cleared, you know because it was Brigitte who did it. And I'm sturdy again on my feet. You just need a coat."

There hanging on a nail was an old coat that Revaz threw over his shoulders and a heavy wool scarf that he put around his neck. So Anzévui leaned against his cane. On one side he had his cane, on the other Revaz; one hand leaned on his thick blackthorn cane, the other arm passed through Revaz's arm, who supported him. In this way he took one step, then another through the dark night. He moved his foot forward then he stopped, then he moved the other foot forward. Revaz said to him, "Be careful there, here's a bump, here's a good place to step, there you go." And no one could see anything and they had no light. Only, that night, all the windows in the village were lit up just in front of them and a little behind them, so much so that the raised edges of the path could be seen a little bit; and the two men moved forward little by little, and you could hear Anzévui sigh every once in a while, and he was coughing. But Revaz said, "We're getting there, we're almost there... and you know he's a brave man, and he'd already started to lose his sight, and we must stop all of this unhappiness from falling on him at one time... be careful! Good, keep going, I've got you... and I also think he must be your age, you know... yes, it's a blood thing... he fell backwards trying to get out of his bed..."

It took two of them to help him up the stairs. Everyone was asked to leave the room; the armchair was pushed to the edge of the bed; we told Anzévui to sit down. He let himself sink down against the back rest; he kept his cane between his legs. The big felt hat with its worn edges was still on his head and two long strands of white hair escaped on one side, hanging down onto his shoulders, and in front his beard hung down to his belly. He watched Old Man Métrailler with his little gray eyes. He watched him a long time without moving (except for his hands which trembled slightly and another slight tremble that moved his beard against his chest); and then:

"Martin!"

"Martin, hey, do you recognize me?"

But the other man still had not moved; so Anzévui looked at him again, nodding his head, after which he said, "Martin, I see what's happened; you just need to let yourself go."

And we watched the old man's body relax all of a sudden; his flexibility came back to him like it does to frozen ground when a warm wind blows across it; he raised his hands a little, his mouth opened like he was going to say something; and his jaw dropped slowly downward which is when we saw that he was dead.

So the old people of the village came, one after the other, to pay their respects, and there were only three or four of them. Meanwhile we could hear the sound of a hammer in the woodworker's workshop.

They stood at the door, they looked toward the bed, they said, "Is that you, Martin Métrailler?"

They walked forward, they picked up the small larch twig from the vase where it was dipped in holy water; and standing in front of the bed, they said, "Goodbye, Martin Métrailler, bon voyage! You were a good man, Martin Métrailler."

They looked at him one last time; he'd been put into his Sunday best, all black clothes.

He'd been put into his Sunday dress shirt, it was a white shirt, and his Sunday tie, it was a silk tie; his hands, which were like two packages of small hard long things wrapped in old newspaper, held a crucifix against his chest.

"You were a good friend."

And then, "You remember, at the big target, the Sunday holiday... well, it's over Métrailler. But it doesn't matter," they told him. "Maybe you're lucky. You've died your own death, died when you wanted to..."

The woodworker had finished putting in the nails. The woodworker began to paint the coffin black. And the next morning, they left for Lower Saint-Martin where the dead are buried in the small cemetery which encircles the church. The frost was still hard; the snow beneath the bearers' footsteps complained like an ailing child. The road had been opened up with a shovel once again; it was bordered in places by walls over a meter high and it wasn't very wide; so they raised the coffin as high as they could and the black box rocked back and forth, looking like a little boat on a little sea amidst the softness of the snow.

Was it to show you the countryside one last time, Métrailler, so vast and beautiful when seen from up here? Was it so that you could see it from above, as if you were soaring, as if you were in the air, like when the bird with his unfurled wings has all that great blue emptiness below him? —but we couldn't see anything, we kept on not being able to see anything. And the ground at the cemetery was still so frozen that, waiting for it to thaw, they had to put the coffin in a great mound of snow and into that they stuck the cross.

SEVEN

"I hammer a nail; that makes fifteen."

It was Sunday again; Follonier reminded himself that it was the next day they were going to go down, and so he had to see Arlettaz to make sure he'd understood.

Years before, Arlettaz's house had been one of the prettiest in the village. Back then he had money; back then he also had a daughter who came and went, which meant that Arlettaz was happy. He'd repainted the shutters on the house; and then when Adrienne was 17 years old, he'd had the kitchen redone. White curtains that were clean and well-ironed and held in red curtain tiebacks could be seen on all the windows; every day a pretty blue smoke rose happily from the chimney and rushed upwards along the slopes to join the blue of the sky above.

Follonier was thinking it had changed, raising his head toward the shutters that were barely hanging on, and the broken windows of the first floor. It's just that before she was there; but now she was no longer there, and everything had changed. The path on the side of the house had not even been cleared; he had to step over a huge pile of snow in which footsteps made a kind of path. Follonier was thinking how things change. He knocked; there was no answer which is what he expected; so much so that after knocking one more time just to soothe his conscience, he leaned against the door handle without a second thought. And yes, Arlettaz was there. It wasn't easy to see him at first because of the darkness; but then we saw the lighter spot of his face turning slowly toward us, and he was seated in front of a bottle of spirits and a glass at a large table covered with all kinds of kitchen utensils and dirty bowls, his hat on his head; because the fire was out.

It seemed that Follonier was used to the place. He simply walked over to Arlettaz, "Well, I see that you're not ready. There's no rush."

He sat down in front of Arlettaz on the other side of the table; then he raised the collar of his jacket saying, "A bit chilly inside, isn't it?" and then, "It's tomorrow you know."

So Arlettaz said, "What?"

"Tomorrow we're going to the notary; he's expecting us. I have the paper."

"Ah!"

"You don't want to come?"

"Yes, I do," Arlettaz said, "I've got nothing left."

"And those hundred francs?"

Arlettaz gestured to the bottle. "We said a thousand francs; you gave me an advance of a hundred; you're only going to give me nine hundred francs, you thief!"

"Nine hundred," Follonier said. "Nine hundred in cash, nine hundred on the table."

"Thief!"

"Nine hundred in bank notes or in coins, as you like."

"Thief!"

"I can see you're not in a good mood this morning... but if we go down, this is what I wanted to say to you, you must... if we're going down, you must get yourself a bit ready. You must shave. And Lamon has hairclippers..."

"What's the point?"

"Of course there's no point, but... well... there are other people."

"I don't care about other people."

"As you like..."

Arlettaz filled his glass again, without even thinking to offer some to Follonier, which is extremely impolite; and so Follonier said, "Okay, it's understood then; I'll pass by and pick you up early to-morrow morning."

Only Arlettaz didn't seem to have heard; he was again in the clouds; he was looking in front of him through his enormous beard into which his ears had disappeared.

He said, "I found her letter; do you remember? I showed you. She dropped it in the post in Martigny..."

He wrestled in the pocket of his vest and eventually pulled out a piece of paper folded four times, all bent at the corners: "I hadn't understood," he was saying.

"You remember, I had gone to look for her at her cousin's in Sion but she was no longer there. And then, it was something like three months later that she wrote me this letter. Why did she write to me?"

He read from the paper: *My dear father, I'm well, I have a good job. I'm writing to tell you not to be worried about me. I'll send a longer letter soon.*

"Stupid!" he said, "I hadn't understood. A beautiful daughter, what can one do with a beautiful daughter?"

"Ah!" he said suddenly, "It's better that she's gone, with what's happening now. And all of this, and you, and me..."

"And this," he gestured to the walls and to everything we could see outside through the windows; he emptied his glass in one swallow, shrugged his shoulders.

"It doesn't matter," said Follonier, "I'll come for you tomorrow morning. And it would be a chance for you to see if maybe you can't find her this time. If you want, we'll go looking for her together when we've finished at the notary..."

Arlettaz said neither yes nor no. Which didn't matter, and the two men left very early the next morning.

Because it was a little brighter outside, Arlettaz's clothing was even more surprising by its contrast against the sharpness of the surrounding snow. It was threadbare, barely held in place; he was wearing two jackets—one brown, the other black—that he had put one on top of the other, and the one above was shorter than the one below. His trousers were torn at the knee and a colorless hat was barely holding on top of his head because his hair was so thick; meanwhile, around his neck, instead of a collar, he'd wrapped a pair of women's stockings. He walked with difficulty, having placed his feet in old shoes that were as wide as they were long, the color of stone, heavy as stone, hard as stone, so much so that he dragged them behind him, not strong enough to lift them up. But what does this matter? And what use is it to be well-dressed, since everything will disappear, you will, I will, and then she will; but the only consolation is that we will go together, she and I, at the same time, all at once; this is what he was thinking while nodding his head, his hands in his pockets, his cane under his arm. They arrived at Lower Saint-Martin; people asked them, "Where are you going?"

"We're having a walk around."

And Arlettaz was already thirsty and would have liked to stop at the inn, "Just quickly for a glass," he said, but Follonier said, "None of that, not before we've been to the notary. You have to be able to see clearly to sign. If you're good, I'll buy you a drink in Sion once we've finished our business." Arlettaz stopped in front of the inn; there were some children there, and they made fun of him. They yelled, "Hey, Mustache Man!" and burst out laughing; "Look at that beard!" and then, because Follonier was turning towards them, they disappeared in all directions making a huge noise like a flock of sparrows.

Arlettaz eventually gave in, Follonier having walked in front of him on the path toward the road where, a little farther on, they got the truck that would take them down to the city.

In the city they went to see the notary. Arlettaz was no longer speaking.

He was asked to sit next to the desk where the notary, holding the paper in his hands, began to read it from behind his glasses, stopping for a long time on the sum that had to be paid:

"One thousand, we have said one thousand."

Arlettaz didn't react. He only said, "I would like to be paid in small bills."

"Well, I'll make change for you," Follonier said, "Fifty franc and twenty franc bills? I'll send my clerk to change the bills. Do you agree? Are you going to sign?"

They both signed the paper.

There were not many people in the streets. They had a drink, then they ate. And then Follonier said, "Now, do you want to go looking for her? Where should we go first?"

Arlettaz didn't know anymore. He said, "I already went everywhere and her cousin is still here, but she laughs when she sees me coming."

He said, "Let's go along the street."

Then he said, "I'll pay for now; let's go looking for her in the cafés because of the serving girls."

They went into the cafés and Arlettaz said to the serving girls, "Where are you from?"

The girls answered, "What business is it of yours?"

"Well," he said, "It's just that my daughter is—I think anyway—working the same kind of job."

"What's her name?"

"Adrienne Arlettaz."

"We don't know her."

"She's a tall girl, much taller than you," Arlettaz was saying, "And bigger too, and then she's also much prettier than you…"

"You're a rude one!"

But he wasn't laughing.

"Twenty-two… she'll be twenty-two at the end of the month… do you want to see her picture?" He took a five-franc coin from his wallet, "Huh?" he was saying, "You see, from the government; hair wrapped three times around her head, and tall and strong, I'm telling you, with a fine carriage…you haven't seen her?"

Some of the girls laughed, the others shrugged their shoulders and turned away; but he fell deeper and deeper beneath the effects of the wine, while he looked in his pockets for his pipe with his blackened hands, couldn't find it, forgot about it; then, growing angry about his pipe he started looking for it again; luckily Follonier was in a good mood and watched over him, making change for him; and then around two o'clock, took him by the arm.

They were lucky. First they were able to get a little truck that brought them to the bottom of the mountain on the other side of the valley; and there they were lucky to find another car that was going up half way to Lower Saint-Martin; they had only another hour to go; and Follonier held on to Arlettaz by the arm, sometimes pulling him forward, sometimes stopping him from falling to the side, because he was no longer sturdy on his legs. Arlettaz was talking, talking the whole time… feeling sorry for himself about his field, reproaching himself for having sold it, then thinking about it no more, thinking of his daughter; then he spoke to the pine trees along the road, telling them that he was all alone. Then he spoke to the crows that were chatting amongst themselves, telling them he was all alone in life. And then it was impossible to tell to whom he was speaking, because the crows had moved into the thickness of the woods. "Oh, it isn't nice," he was saying, "but luckily it's all coming to an end."

"Good day," he said, "Or maybe it's goodnight. Hello, lamps!"

Because they had just begun to appear in the far-off windows of Lower Saint-Martin. "And who are you?" he said, "But you'll burn out soon—that's the end of it, of all of you, just like us."

"Be quiet," said Follonier, "We're arriving."

"Thief!" Arlettaz said. And then, "Well, if it were possible, she'd be there, wouldn't she, and not you; you're too ugly, you're too fat, you're too badly put together. Imagine if she were coming back! I would have gone to look for her; she would have done half the road and I would have done the other half; and we'd see from far that it was her just by the way she holds her head."

"We're here," said Follonier.

Arlettaz began to cry; he took off the women's stockings that were wrapped around his neck because he was too hot.

He laughed because he'd seen the light at the inn; he started to cry again. And then, standing in front of the door, he called out to everyone (this was at five o'clock in the evening, in Lower Saint-Martin); he was saying, "Come on! Come on everyone! I'm paying. I have money, I have too much. Because how much longer is this going to last? Hey, Follonier, where are you? He's a thief, you know... my field in Empeyres," he was saying, "It was a beautiful field..."

We brought him inside. "Who can say otherwise? The most beautiful field in the region, a full acre in a single piece, with the best sun and so close to the village; an acre of good early rye: and do you know how much he gave me for it? Thief, where are you?"

We came over to him, he said, "Let's go in, it's on me. Hey, Follonier!"

But Follonier had disappeared, which made Arlettaz laugh.

And to show that you could trust him, he pulled all of the bills from his pocket, nearly nine hundred francs in small bills, which made lots of little bits of paper.

He held them in his hand, and he said, "Well, let's get going, there's only fifteen days left. How many of you are there? Count yourselves!" And then to the innkeeper, "Hey, boss, ten liters..."

Around midnight, the innkeeper, who had been busy closing up the place, went into the stable; he gave a kick to the legs of the cow, and he gave a kick to the belly of the mule, and in this way he made a space just there for Arlettez, between the cow and the mule.

EIGHT

As for Métrailler, he was thinking he needed to set himself straight about something. Because since his father's passing, he could only think of one thing and that was that Anzévui must have thrown a curse on the old man. So he decided he would go to see Anzévui and he would make him explain what it was all about.

He headed out a little after noon. He ran into Brigitte along the way; she was just returning home.

"Where are you going," she asked him.

He didn't answer her.

And so then she, turning towards him as he passed in front of her, said, "Come on, Métrailler, don't torment yourself; everything is okay... and don't upset him either, you know, because he's weakening. I swept up around the house; you'll find him beneath his plants. Go quietly."

Métrailler was not listening to her. He knocked at the door, he went inside. He saw the fire. Anzévui was seated in a straw armchair with an old cushion behind his back; his head was leaning forward because of its weight, his beard dangling on his knees.

"What do you want?"

"I wanted to see you, sir."

"Well?"

"And speak to you."

"Well, then," said Anzévui, "sit down."

He coughed.

The plants were held by their roots to the beams and hung, head down, like bats.

In front of Anzévui was a table; on the table, there was the book; it was covered with marbled red parchment like those soaps we once used for doing laundry at the fountain.

Métrailler said, "So then. Was it you?"

"What?"

"Yes," said Métrailler, "You came and then he died."

"And you," said Anzévui, "won't you die as well?"

Métrailler waited a moment, needing to think; he started again, "But maybe he wouldn't have died if you hadn't come. They said that you were going to heal him and Revaz told me that you healed his knee…"

"He obeyed."

"Oh," said Métrailler, "I know he wasn't doing well and that the doctor couldn't do anything for him, but people say that you're wiser than the doctors: and so, instead of fixing him, you let him be unfixed."

"It was written."

"But listen here, Father Antoine, because they're also saying that you're going to stop the moon and the stars and that the sun is never going to come back; so I thought, if you have power over the stars, you must have more than enough power over men and that you could make them die as well as make them healthy."

Anzévui said, "It isn't me. It's in the book."

He coughed. And again he lowered his head, and his beard went with it, rustling against his chest like a thin trickle of water on a bed of broken slate.

"I obey. All I do is read what is written. I saw that your father's time was up. He was like a man hanging onto a branch to keep from being pulled away by the water; I told him, 'let it all go.'"

The flame from the fire was on his face and then was no longer there; there were shadows around his eyes like water in the scoop of a rock.

Métrailler said nothing else; Anzévui also said nothing. Then Anzévui coughed.

And so Métrailler said, "Well, it's just that I went up there."

"Where?"

"Up the mountain, to Grand-Dessus."

"Why?"

"To see if the sun wasn't there anymore; and it was still there, but..."

"It's because it's swinging." Anzévui coughed. "It isn't me. It's in the book." He took the book up onto his knees, while the flame of the fire weakened, growing smaller like it was about to go out; and he said, "I can't see anymore. Métrailler, add some wood."

There were small pieces of wood stacked at the base of the wall. "Put some kindling first, and then those big logs that hold the fire."

And so we see him again with his deep wrinkles across his forehead, his long hair, his white beard, his little eyes were shining like they'd just been washed in cool water; and having begun to turn the pages of the book, he said, "It's written in here... let them laugh, if they want to laugh. We're going to be like the moon that has only one side visible; we're going to be on the dark side."

"It was red," said Cyprien: "it was like a severed head. There was all this blood around it."

"It's because it's going to go out. Everything will swing. And, the rest of us, we won't see it anymore because we're going to be on the side of the earth where it'll be night time all the time."

"When will it happen?"

"Soon. You see, it's written here. I counted it up. That makes 37."

He showed a page with black letters in two columns and a big margin on which could be seen many symbols and numbers printed in red: the moon, the sun, the signs of the zodiac.

"I counted, recounted, and recounted again, then I counted even one more time: it makes 37, and then four, and then it has to make 12 or 13, which is exactly the date when the sun should be coming back to us. And well, it won't come back. And so instead of becoming brighter that day, it'll be darker, and even darker, and always more dark. A change in the axis. It's that the earth turns in the air," he said.

And then he was out of breath.

"And so it won't turn anymore. Right now it's still turning in two ways, but then it'll only turn in one direction."

"And then?"

"And then it'll be night, it'll be night for us. We'll have to light our lamps all day. It'll be cold, always more cold. What's the temperature today? Three or four above zero? And at the beginning of April it's usually over four."

"Well," he said, "it'll be -10 and then -20. Water will be like rock, the trees will split in two, we will have to break our cheese with an ax, and the bread will be hard like a millstone."

And so Métrailler began to be afraid. He watched Anzévui and his labored breathing; Anzévui opened his mouth. Anzévui coughed, coughed again, and since the fire had died down again his eyes were like the eyes of a dead man.

He managed to catch his breath, he said, "This is what's written."

"And so," Métrailler said, "it was good that my poor father let himself go?"

"He obeyed."

"And the rest of us, what are we to do?"

"You all must obey as well."

"That's all?"

"That's all."

Anzévui slipped the book out from where it rested on his knees because it was a heavy book and the weight of it made him tired. Inside the book was the entire past, the entire present, the entire future: that makes a heavy book. This was in February; it was even already the 25th of February. Métrailler said goodbye to Anzévui: it was the time of year in those luckier countries that the first flowers were opening, and there were places even in these other countries where the sap is already running in the vines. Down there, where Revaz's son had gone, on those walls turned toward the south, maybe there was already sun and maybe there were those golden or purple grapes hanging in the cracks of the stone. The blue is above you: there are three kinds of blue—the water, the mountain and the sky. He was thinking about this first spring, thinking about when the sky has finally split in two; and in the angle of a wall, well into the shadows, a small peach tree like a bit of pink cotton, like the kind under a pair of earrings a man buys for his sweetheart; I don't have one anymore, but it's no matter. But will it be like that for them down there? Just like for us? Will the light go out at once for them as it will for us? Because at least for now they are in the sun and enjoying it; in the light and the full light; in the colors, in all kinds of colors; for us it's gray and black; for us it's six months of gray and black; for us it's the middle of October to the middle of April with no change (he raised his head): not up above, not below, and not in the middle either. It will weaken, leaving a feeble light; there won't be any more light at all; nothing anywhere; and, looking at the houses of the village, he thought how they wouldn't be there anymore; I won't be here, we won't be here.

Just then he saw a little girl who was kneeling down before a wooden cross. The cross stood in the bend of the path leading to Anzévui's from the village path.

The cross was held up by a pile of stones; the little girl had brushed the snow off with a corner of her apron; then she'd kneeled down.

From closer up, Métrailler saw that it was little Lucienne Emonet. She was maybe eight years old, but she was already wearing a long dress like an adult. She was like a little woman. She wore, like all the women, a black kerchief on her head, a shawl knotted around her waist, and heavy hobnailed shoes like all the women on the mountain.

She didn't see him coming; Métrailler stopped and wondered what she was doing there. And he waited for her to stand up before joining her.

"What are you doing? You're going to get yourself all wet."

"But no!"

There was a bit of flour on her checked apron; she brushed it off.

"You see, it's already gone."

It's that it was still cold and the snow was as dry as road dust on the objects around; only Lucienne's hands were wet, red and covered in chillblains, but a little girl's hands are always like this on the mountain.

And Métrailler said to her again, "Did I interrupt you?"

"Of course not, I didn't even know you were there."

They walked next to one another; suddenly Métrailler asked her, "Is there something wrong?"

"Oh, yes there is!"

"What is it?"

"It's my Aunt Justine."

"Is she ill?"

"No, not her, but she has a baby and she's worried about him."

"Why?"

"Because he's really little and she says he's going to die."

"Ah!" said Métrailler.

"She says that we're all going to die because the sun is going away. She says it isn't fair. And that, if it's fair for the old people and the men and the older women, it isn't at all fair for the little children who've never done anything to anyone."

"So," said Métrailler, "You came to pray to the sun?"

"Oh, no!"

"It's too bad," Métrailler continued, "It's not the right time; it's not the weather for it . The sun is hiding; it didn't see you, it couldn't hear you; we can't even tell where it is today, it's so far away from us."

"But, you know," she said, "It isn't the sun."

"Then who is it?"

"It's the good Lord."

"Ah!"

"Yes," she said, "because it's God who controls the sun. He would bring the sun back if He wanted; and He would want to, wouldn't He?"

Suddenly, Métrailler felt free; his whole body felt light and he thought, "What am I ever thinking? I've lost my mind. It's this bad weather giving me ideas, it's Anzévui; it's being cooped up too long without doing anything all day. It's the women, because it's in their nature to believe everything they hear; it's the old people, because they're unwell…"

"Of course," Isabelle said.

She burst out laughing and threw back her head; the underside of her chin moved like a pigeon's throat. Because he was looking up at her. He had continued along his way; he was passing just in front of her house. She was on the front step, and he was below her, standing in the middle of the path.

She burst out laughing because she'd asked him, "Where are you coming from?" and he'd said, "From Anzévui's house."

"But of course not, it's nothing but old women's stories, but come up a moment and warm yourself. I'm alone; it's my husband, my crazy old husband…"

"Where is he?"

"He went to get wood, he's behaving like Brigitte; he told me, 'She's right, she's a woman who sees into the future.' He went with Jean and the sled to get some wood."

Métrailler went in. It was warm. There was an oven. It was a well-equipped kitchen, and up-to-date. It was new. It was a new house. It was made from a lovely varnished larch that gleamed, with knots like eyes, with veins like on a man's arms. Isabelle had switched on the electric lamp that hung over the table in a pink paper shade with fine pleats, "Do you really think he could be that stupid, my poor Augustin, my silly husband. He doesn't want to discuss it. He says, 'You never know.'"

"And Jean?"

"Oh, it makes him laugh, but he's got a good heart. And you know, he's the youngest, and he's not yet an adult. They've already gone out six times."

She said, "Have a drink; they won't be too long now."

She had gone into the cellar to fill up a clear glass carafe that showed the color of the wine, and it's a color that is immediately familiar. Métrailler gestured to the carafe, "And well," he said, "the sun... doesn't it look like it's already come back?"

The wine was lovely to see, it's a beginning; and now he looked at Isabelle. "And you're also lovely to see. And you've preserved it for us, you've done the right thing."

"Well, because I love it..."

"You've done the right thing, you see, and it's good to have it in front of the eyes again, otherwise we'd lose hope."

And he looked at her, "It's just that you take the sun well. And I don't. The sun bronzes you; but it burns me."

"Well, maybe there are those it loves and those it doesn't love."

"I stay as gray as a stone or I become as red as a crawfish. My skin splits like the earth in a garden. But it ripens and rounds you; it dries me out, it hollows me out. And yet God knows the sun should know me, since I've been walking out close to him, up there on the mountain, among the rocks, and on the snow, and on the ice, and never with a sun shade; but maybe you're right, maybe the sun has its favorites."

"Well, it's because us women," she said, "we're in the pastures, we're at the harvest, we're working the rake and the pitchfork. We're in the green. We're amidst the grasshoppers; he watches us over the pine trees. Oh, he isn't so sweet with all the girls... I pretend not to notice; he says, 'Is that you?' and I tell him, 'Yes, it's me.' I turn my back to him; so he comes up, he tickles me, to show a girl that he's there, on the arms, the shoulders, the back..."

She was seated at the table; she was speaking over her shoulder.

"We women ask him for nothing; we only take what he gives us; which is why he's so good to us."

"And maybe he wants to do us, us men, he wants to do us wrong," said Métrailler.

She flashed her teeth, which shone in the lamplight, she showed the tip of her tongue as she wet her lips, at the same time dipping her head like a shy little girl.

"That's why you were afraid. Oh, you're not the only one! But you're not afraid anymore, are you? No one can be afraid when they're with me... To your health, Métrailler."

Because she had a glass for herself; she raised it; and all the while she was pressing on the table with her other hand. "Because it's almost all over, soon we'll know what it's all about; and everyone else, too, the poor dears."

"Who do you mean?"

"You know, Denis Revaz, his wife, Brigitte, Justine Emonet, Morand, Lamon."

She continued, "And Augustin... and then Arlettaz of course, because he's drinking everything."

"He's got money for drinking?"

"Of course, he sold his last field to Follonier."

"Oh, that Follonier is a clever fox."

"Clever indeed," she said, "because he got it for half its value. You see? And every night someone has to carry the poor man back to his house, because he says he's got to hurry if he doesn't want to leave any money behind him..."

"To whom?"

She said, "To the devil, and he's got nothing but time, and Pralong doesn't refuse him."

Then she started to laugh again, "A person shouldn't have kids if they aren't able to keep them. What do you say, Métrailler?"

Then, all of a sudden, "A man shouldn't take a wife if he doesn't know..."

Then she quieted; and sat at the table, beneath the lamp with the pink lampshade that lit up the nape of her neck, and it's lovely to see, her chignon which threw off its blue-tinged highlights, and slowly the line of her downy cheek or the corner of her eyelid and her eyes shining:

"He loved her a lot, you know (she was speaking now of Arlettaz), only he didn't know how to love. A person has to know how. And us, you know, us girls, it's maybe not that kind of love that we need; yes, that type of love. He didn't know how. She was a bit older than me, about three or four years older than me. How old do you think I am, Métrailler?"

Her hands flat on the table, beneath the lamp, an evening when night is drawing near already, even if already the night is coming later:

"I'm not even 19, maybe I married too young. Augustin is twenty-three: he's four years older than me. He's the same age as Arlettaz's daughter. Oh, I remember her well. Her name was Adrienne; and we were little girls and she was a big girl, but she told us she was so bored. And we asked her, 'Why are you bored?' 'Because everything is so small here.' Listen, Métrailler, you're a reasonable man, do you think it's too small here? Do you think that at 23 years old, a person is already an old man?"

But there was a noise in front of the house; it was the soft thud of footsteps and a low whistle: the rails of the heavy sled in the snow.

Métrailler went to look out the window; but she stayed seated at the table until they came in, having emptied their load into the shed; and Augustin was thin and pale with thinning straight hair, Jean was tan, his cheeks were red, his eyes lively and his hair curly.

It was clear that Augustin was worried, he said, "What are you doing here? Oh, I see; you're drinking while the rest of us work; we're all sweaty and freezing; we've got our shirt stuck to our back with sweat but we can't feel the tip of our fingers..."

She said, "Jean, go get two glasses."

She had stayed in her seat; Augustin flopped down onto the edge of the bench, then fell forward with the top half of his body, his elbows up, shaking his head.

And Métrailler said to him, "Where are you coming from like that?"

"Where am I coming from? Is that a question? We've only got fifteen days left. Go ask Brigitte how her stocks are. She got started in time... she knew what to do. We're going to need wood, won't we, if we're going to hold out."

NINE

Before ten o'clock the next morning, he was already seated in front of his empty pint glass. He tapped the table with the bottom of the glass; Fat Sidonie came over.

And Fat Sidonie went to fill up his pint and then wrote the amount he owed on a slate; which by nightfall had made a large sum because everyone had been drinking on Arlettaz's tab for some time now.

But he was the one who wanted this. He pulled a roll of bills from his pocket, "We've got to use this up, otherwise I'll leave it behind and what's the use? When it's night, no use at all, not to anyone."

It's just that the season was moving forward, it's just that the nice weather was coming. Me, I'm waiting.

He was alone. The wireless wasn't on. It wasn't yet time for the room to fill up. He was there, seated, letting things pass, silent, unmoving, lighting his pipe from time to time, letting it go out, then lighting it again through the pewter lid with its holes that he would forget to lift up; and his fingers shook so much that the flame strolled all about the bowl and never managed to stay steady upon it.

Follonier came in. "Hey, there, how's it going?"

Follonier sat down facing Arlettaz. Arlettaz didn't answer.

Follonier was in a good mood, "You're lucky, Arlettaz. What a good deal you made."

"Thief!" And at the same time, he tapped the table with the bottom of the bottle. "Another one, and another glass!"

That was how it went. While we waited for the change of season, we all drank more at Pralong's, and on credit.

"Thief!" said Arlettaz.

"We know all about it," Follonier said.

"Well, I'm calling you a thief all the same. A field that my mother gave me! And not only from my mother, but from my mother's father, and from his father... (but he was getting it mixed up); the most beautiful field in the parish, the flattest, with the best sun, and not a single stone, you know, because it was sifted by hand, again and again...Anyway, it's all over. Because it's all over, isn't it?"

"Of course it's all over."

"So, we'll drink."

"Did you go to Le Bouveret like you said you were going to?"

"To Le Bouveret?"

"To look for your daughter? You don't remember? You said you'd already been everywhere but there."

"Not worth it anymore..." Arlettaz said. "Because we'll see each other again... because the sun, you know, it isn't just for us that it's going away, not just for us up here in Upper Saint-Martin, don't you know? But for everyone?"

Follonier nodded.

"For everyone in Lower Saint-Martin, too, right? And everyone in the valley? And the people on the lake? Good. So..."

"So?"

"So, for her too... Adrienne and I will see each other again, won't we? That'll be the right time, so what's the use of running about?"

The boys came in, the young men, and Pralong too.

"Because we're going to find each other..."

They started drinking. They looked at Arlettaz; his beard and his hair had grown even longer. And as they grew, they became like a frame, his face grew smaller and smaller, more wrinkled, like an apple at the end of winter. He was still wearing his two jackets, one on top of the other, but the sleeves of the one on top were open at the sides, hanging down and showing the other jacket underneath. This made it look like he had put brown cuffs on, even if he was wearing a black suit, like for some kind of wedding. But without a collar and maybe even without a shirt or even the tatters of a shirt, but he didn't even know it himself, because he'd stopped undressing some time ago. And the men were watching him, even if he wasn't looking at anyone; he was looking at something right through us, like we were made of glass, like he couldn't see us.

"It'll be the right time," he said.

Then he began to smile to himself, or was he smiling at what he was seeing?

He asked, "How will it be?"

"It'll be lovely," said Follonier.

They were all around him.

"Will we be changed?"

"Of course, and not just changed, but transfigured... Transfigured, that means we won't have the same face."

"Oh," he said, "She won't need to have hers changed."

"You're the one who'll be changed, you'll be nice to look at. Hey, think about it, Arlettaz, you'll be young!"

And one of the young men said, "And you'll be shaved!"

Another said, "You'll have a hair cut!"

Another, "Well dressed."

"Now, now," Follonier said, "Can't you lot be serious for once? Listen, Arlettaz, do you remember what the scripture says? It says we'll be together in heaven, everyone, forever. So you're right, you'll find her..."

But it was clear that Arlettaz was a little worried. He said, "How will we recognize each other?"

"By the light," said Follonier. "We've lived so long in shadows. And suddenly there will be light, so much more light than we've ever had here; it'll make us new, renewed. And this light will bring us all together."

"And they'll be angels," said Lucien Revaz.

"Of course," the boys said.

"The sun, you understand, our sun, well, it's nothing. It has spots; it's just the beginning of a sun—an experiment, an imitation, a fake sun, it's nothing at all…"

And because they saw that Arlettaz was already quite lost to the wine and they didn't need to worry about him, they said, "How old are you?"

"Fifty-two."

"Well, you'll be twenty. And how old is she?"

"She'll be twenty-three on May 10th."

"She'll be 18, because that's the most beautiful age; you'll be like two sweethearts."

"Be quiet, boys!"

Only Follonier had also started to laugh; and anyway, it was clear the boys were too far gone and there was no stopping them, and they continued, "It's just that we remember her, we do, and we knew her well, and it isn't our fault she didn't stay here. What can you do, Mr. Arlettaz, she was too beautiful, she was too beautiful for us. But where we'll all be soon, there won't be any more differences between us. Everyone will be young, everyone will be happy. In the paintings…"

They elbowed each other beneath the table.

"You know the ones, in the church… well, yes, she'll have wings; she'll be like an angel… she'll recognize you from above and afar. And she'll come down from above…"

One of them said, "Red and gray like a redstart."

Another, "Green, red and yellow like a goldfinch."

And yet another, "Black and white like a magpie."

But then they saw two fat tears running slowly down old Arlettaz's face like sap on the trunk of a peach tree.

They were silent now; they weren't moving; there were only those two tears that had so much trouble to go down his wrinkled and rough old skin.

Ten

Mr. Revaz called his wife

He was seated in their bedroom at a small table with a lid that went down into a writing desk; he made his wife sit down beside him.

"Listen, we don't know what's going to happen, so we need to get our affairs in order. First you need to write to Julien and tell him to come home."

This was the one of their two sons who worked in the vineyards.

"Write and tell him to arrange for a few days off."

"Yes," he continued, "I'd like him to be here, if anything goes wrong."

Mr. Revaz looked ill, even if his knee was healed. His face was gray, his body too heavy: his cheeks were soft and shadowed with a beard.

"Ah!" he began again, "We've worked hard, haven't we, my dear? Remember all the times we woke up early in the summer, and went to bed late, sometimes working fifteen hours; and think of all the running around we did, how many times a year from here to the summer chalet and from here to the vineyards down below? And now's the time we would have started to enjoy the fruits of all that work... it's just too bad!"

She looked at him in surprise; she was also pale and heavy. She'd never heard him speak so much at one time; and he'd lifted up the lid of the desk.

"OK, you understand you're to write to Julien immediately. And there's also Alphonsine (this was their daughter) but she's married and best she should stay with her husband... we'll be the four of us, we'll be together and everything is in order... I've split the money in three."

He opened a drawer, he took our three bundles tied with string and upon each one he'd written the name of one of his children.

"I've given each their share. No reason the law will need to be involved... and for the house and the land, everything is written down here."

He took a yellow envelope from the drawer, upon which was written, *Last will and testament.*

"This is so you know what you'll need to do, in case I'm the one who goes first."

"But," she said, "Aren't we all going to go together, isn't that...?" She hesitated, "Or no one will go... it's not like you're sick... Listen, Denis, do you really believe all this?"

"You never know. Have you got provisions?"

"Oh, yes," she said, "We've got butter for three months and cheese for six... and I've had bread made for eight. We have three hams, sixty sausage links, twenty-five cured sausages. Eighteen kilos of sugar..."

She thought a moment, then, "A good sack of polenta, and there's enough silage to feed the animals until July..."

"That's good," he said, "because we won't be able to go out anymore."

"Go out?"

"We won't be able to leave the house."

"Why not?"

"Because it'll be dark, and it'll be too cold."

"Who told you this?"

"Anzévui... because until now we've had night, but there was also the day; until now it could be dark but then it was lighter; and there won't be anything but nighttime and more night and only night, and it'll be eight degrees below zero, and then fifteen, then twenty... you have enough wood?"

"Come on," she said, "you know we do, we don't know where to put it anymore. It's piled up against every wall of the house."

"We have to be able to reach it..."

"The woodpile is full, the shed is full."

"You should make a pile in the kitchen; it's safer... And then get us some warm clothes ready, all that you can find for us for clothes and we'll put them one on top of the other as we need to."

He thought some more, and then said, "I think that's all."

It wasn't yet two o'clock; they had already lit the lamp, even if the room was south-facing. And they stayed there beside one another without saying another word, while Mrs. Revaz stared at the lid of the desk—because of the way the wood was laid, the grain looked like a sheaf of wheat —and at the trembling of those soft heavy hands that were too pale. Why had they grown so pale?

Just then, someone came into the kitchen. The first thing Revaz did was close the lid of the desk; then he thought that it must be Lucien.

He called out, "Lucien!"

And Lucien opened the door and looked with surprise at his mother and his father seated under the lamp that was in front of the desk.

"I've put my affairs in order," he said. "It's just in case... anyway, you know."

Lucien said, "No, I don't know."

"Oh, well, it doesn't matter… I divided everything up. There are three bundles. There is one for you, one for your brother, and one for your sister. And I've already shown your mother where they are…"

"Yes," he continued, "You have to plan ahead for troubles. And if your mother… well, you'll know… here, you see."

He showed him the bundles. Then he said, "This is yours… your names are written on them."

He closed the drawer.

"And what are you doing right now?"

"I was just repairing the harrow."

"There's no rush," said Revaz. "It would be better for you to go get more wood."

But Lucien was only thinking of one thing and it was that they had money, that his father was much richer than he thought. He'd never spoken to Lucien of what he might have, but this time he'd seen the envelope… he wanted to go quickly tell Gabrielle.

He had taken the axe, then having hidden it at the base of a tree in the woods that bordered the road, he'd run down to Lower Saint-Martin.

Not far from the village, he'd run into a child and given him ten centimes. "You know where Gabrielle Dussex lives? Well, go tell her that I'm waiting for her, but don't tell anyone but her. If you do this for me, there'll be another ten centimes for you."

The child took off running. And while he waited Lucien kept thinking what a large bundle it was. How much was in there? Bills? And so we'll be rich!

He went to sit down in front of a hay barn upon a pile of cross beams. From where he was sitting, he could look down on Lower

Saint-Martin. From where he was sitting, you see the village in its scoop beneath you, and in this season it looked like the collapsed base of a glacier—meaning that it was filled with ravines.

This is good, Lucien was thinking. I'll ask my father to give me an advance; he can't refuse me. Only, is she going to come? She must be angry since I told her we couldn't see each other like we wanted. But he saw that she was coming anyway. He saw that there are moments in life when everything is upended and a thing looks like its opposite. She appeared below him and came forward as a dark shadow along the path that was also marked with dark shadows, because of the sled rails and marks from shoes. Every once in a while she turned her head toward the village; then she continued to walk forward anyway, which made him stand up and raise his hat.

"You see, all the trouble, well, it's all over..." he said. Then, "Come quickly... hey, Gabrielle!"

Then he yelled out loud, "Come quickly, so I can explain..."

The girl, we saw that she was slender and graceful, a little shy, a little impish, slender and tall. She stopped, she smiled beneath her kerchief.

And he said, "You came anyway, you weren't afraid you'd be seen?"

"Oh," she said, "Why not? Am I doing something forbidden?"

"I had to speak with you," he said, "It's good news, but where can we go to speak quietly."

"We can just go inside the haybarn; it's ours."

She went to get the key hidden in one of the roof beams; they left the door open, they sat down in the hay.

"You see, my father is upset by what people have been talking about. Do you know about it? No. It doesn't matter. But anyway, for some time now he didn't want to hear anything about this marriage... but, you know, that's all going to change."

"When?"

"Soon, in a week or two, around the 12ᵗʰ or the 13ᵗʰ. Because Father is scared, but he'll see soon enough that there wasn't anything to be afraid about. And then, well, there's the money."

She had untied the ends of her kerchief and thrown them behind her shoulders; you could see that she was blonde with fine soft hair knotted in a chignon at the nape of her neck. She was listening without really understanding.

And he said, "I have to tell you everything... you see, I believed it, too, for awhile."

"Believed what?"

The hay behind them was crackling softly; was it the grasshoppers bundled inside or the long plastic ties which were folded in two and stretching out with a snap?

"Do you know old man Anzévui?"

"Of course, we go to him for his remedies."

"Well, he's a wise man, he reads big books all day long. And once he said to my father... oh, he did his calculations, he calculated and re-calculated. And my father believed him. And you?"

"And you?"

"Not me, but my father told me I had to wait. So I ended up thinking as well that we'd have to wait. Because I was scared, too. Then I was dressed as a girl..."

She opened her eyes wide.

"I went as a girl, I borrowed Sidonie's skirt and vest—you know the one, she works at Pralong's. It was a whole group of us. We thought we'd play a joke on Anzévui. They told me, 'You'll be the girl...' So, yes, I was the girl, with flour and then a match head for my eyebrows. Are you angry? Just wait, Gabrielle, just let me tell you... Because we got to his house, the others were hidden, and I'm the one who knocked at the window. And he was there, seated at his fire. It was midnight. I said, 'It's me, Mr. Anzévui.' I faked a girl's voice. I said, 'Open up, Mr. Anzévui; I need your help.' I knocked again at the window. And up to then he'd been seated before his fire, with his back to me, but then he got up. He changed color, he was white to me then. It was his beard. But then I got scared because he was like a cloud..."

"What did you do?"

"I ran off..."

Then he said, "You see, it was upsetting, I thought he wasn't a man, thought he was no longer a man; I was upset."

"And now?"

"Well, this is just what I came to tell you. I don't believe these stories anymore, but my father still believes. So he put his affairs in order; he made three bundles, you know there are three of us, my brother, my sister, and me. And just now he told me—here's yours—and so I saw it; it's thick. I don't know what's inside, it must be bills; and, okay, I don't know if they're thousands or fifties, but there's definitely a pile, there was a lot. We're going to be able to get married."

She was smiling; she said, "But why did you change?"

"Because they made fun of me."

"Who did?"

"The other fellows. Métrailler, Tissières."

"And what else?"

"And also the money, this afternoon. That made me happy, that encouraged me. It just can't go wrong if we know that we'll have some. Don't you think?"

"Well," she said. "It isn't really the money, but you, because of all this time I haven't seen you."

"I didn't dare, I was sad."

"It's forgotten, because you're here."

But he kept on, "I was... well, I knew that we had our own house, fields, pastures, vines; I couldn't not know it because we work these lands, but money... well, we'll also have money. We're going to be able to make it official."

"Let's wait."

"Why wait? I mean, yes, if you want, until the 13th, because it's the 13th... But, hey, don't you think it's a strange story? I mean, the weather we've had this winter. And of course we don't see the sun up here for six months and down here where you are not much longer, but it doesn't matter, the problem is that we haven't had any good weather, not once, not since October, not a clear sky even once, we haven't had a single day without fog; so the old people, the women, the poorly... and this crazy old man with his books..."

"Well," she said, "Maybe it's that this particular sun isn't the only one that matters. There's more than one, you know."

"Where is it, this other one?"

She smiled and dipped her head; she brought her hand to the left side of her chest.

ELEVEN

Isabelle asked Jeanne Emery the seamstress to come; it was Friday.

They set themselves up in the upstairs room. Jeanne Emery had brought her sewing machine with her. A nice fire was burning in the wood stove that had been lit that morning.

Isabelle placed a box on the table which had been pushed up against the window because of the poor daylight; and opening it, she said, "Is there enough, can you do it?"

"My goodness!"

It was a large swathe of blue alpaca wool; in its folds were lovely hints of silver.

"I asked Augustin to let me write to Anthamatten to ask for cloth; and can you believe he didn't want to. The first time he's ever said no."

"What's wrong with him?"

She touched her forehead; then placed a finger over her lips. "You can't say anything; it's pure silliness. What can you do? He thinks of nothing but his wood. He left again for the woods this morning, with Jean..."

"Well then," said Jeanne Emery. "We can still take measurements. Let's see how much cloth we need for the skirt and we'll see if we have enough for the bodice."

"It's so odd," said Isabelle, "This is the first time Augustin has refused me something. And I'm a girl who knows how to get her way. I told him it was for spring, and that spring was coming. He just shrugged his shoulders. He doesn't look well: there are five or six of them looking poorly in the village. You know why. And I even said to him, 'Don't you think it's up to us, to the women, to start making ourselves beautiful? That will encourage the weather.' And he told me to be quiet, that I didn't know what I was talking about. And I said, 'Come on, Augustin, come here.' I said, 'Is the answer still no?' To start I gave him a kiss on the tip of his nose waiting for him to say yes and waiting for it all to change; but it didn't change. So, oh well!"

Jeanne Emery had taken her measuring ribbon. Isabelle took off her shirt. The room brightened as if the sun had already returned.

It seemed that we were suddenly two months into the good season.

"Say," said Jeanne Emery, "It isn't just your face... I say, it isn't just your face that's so tan. How do you do it?"

"I don't do anything."

"87"

This was the length of the skirt.

"You want it short, don't you?"

"Yes, when it's short, it's easier to go dancing in the summer chalet."

Jeanne Emery wrote the numbers in her notebook.

69. This was the size of her waist.

"Your waist is so slender!" she said.

"What can I say? It isn't my fault. He's so lazy," she said, "And a bit awkward. It's been eight months, hasn't it? What should I do? Yes, eight months we've been married. I even said to Augustin, 'The children should come in the summer, they should come when the weather is nice, if we want them to enjoy it...' And now there won't be a child before next winter; and maybe there won't ever be one. Jeanne Emery, I'm telling you to make my skirt short."

They were good friends, even if Jeanne was a little older than Isabelle, and friends tell each other everything.

"Make me a young girl's skirt and we can start dancing again up in the summer chalets…"

"With who?"

"With anyone. Will you come, Jeanne?"

"Wait," said Jeanne, "I have to measure the fabric now."

"That's three and a half meters."

"Wait, one, two, three; not exactly. And we'll need two and a half meters for the skirt… I won't have a full meter left over."

She came with her cloth measuring tape, and Isabelle said, "Darn, it's cold!" while Jeanne placed it on her skin from her neck to her shoulder, and then from her shoulder to her wrist.

"It's just that you're so curvy! I won't have anything to make the collar with."

"So don't make one."

"What would people say?"

"I have my scarves, no one will see a thing," she said, "Anyway, I have all sorts of things; from when we were courting, when he still gave me presents, when we went to the fair together."

She went down the stairs; she came back up with a little shell-covered box, the big ones glued to the lid, the smaller ones on the side; she carried it with both hands; with a gold clasp and lock, "This, too, is from when we were courting."

Inside the box there were silk handkerchiefs folded into fours, a gold broach, earrings, a coral necklace, hair pins, copper combs.

"See, I can manage it, because we had good weather once. But it'll come back; we'll make it come back if it doesn't want to… Listen, Jeanne, cut the skirt; for the rest, we'll figure it out. When can I try it?"

"Sunday afternoon, if you want."

"At your house?"

"At my house if you want."

"I think it's better," said Isabelle, "I prefer he doesn't know."

She tried her kerchiefs on before the mirror; in the mirror she was a sun. She made a lovely color in the mirror that was reflected back toward her and around her: she was the color of a peach, like a muscat grape at the end of the season. She folded them diagonally and put the squares of silk around her neck; they had fringes, the fringes were curly, and between the fringes we saw her skin.

And Jeanne Emery said, "How do you make your hair so shiny?"

"I wash it with baking soda."

"And then what do you do?"

"I dry it before the fire."

I hammer a nail, it's the last one; And then, Brigitte thought, I won't move anymore.

She had gone again to change the oil in the lamp; she had trimmed the wick, she went back to sit down and then she reminded herself that she would be ready when the time came, but she wondered what it would be like.

It was still dark in the village; there was not the slightest noise anywhere, not outside the house, not inside; she had gathered her hands together in her lap, she leaned her head, making a silence inside of herself. On the 13th when there was a fire on the mountain, there won't be anything. In three days. I'm not moving. Long ago it was green up there, it was yellow, it was pink; and all of a sudden it was like throwing an armful of wood on the fire: well, it'll be gray, and the gray will grow darker, and always darker. I'm not moving. I will learn.

I will light my fire, I have a full bottle of oil: and I will stay calm until the night: but it won't be completely night for me, not right away, because I'll have my lamp lit and it'll last as long as I will.

Anzévui said that it'll be cold and always colder, but I'll have my fire; it'll last as long as I have the strength to stretch my arms.

As long as my heart beats, as long as the old blood in my body keeps its warmth beneath my old skin;—then, by Your will, because You decide it all, because You see, I won't defend myself, I won't protest, I won't fight, I won't argue; and the flame of the lamp will be there to announce that You are coming, entering slowly into each house one after the other, and then into mine.

She closed her eyes, she opened them again; it was time to go down to mass. She wrapped herself in her shawl, she wrapped a black wool cloth around her head; she took her hymnal, and at the same time, opening a drawer, she took four small hard round objects, each wrapped in a piece of newsprint, and she put them in her pocket. She didn't walk fast, which was why she left early; and so she was alone on the path. It was cleared now and well trod, because it hadn't snowed in a while. And, even when the snow doesn't melt, as the season advances, it compacts and always more, always decreasing its depth; so that it became easier to get around, and because of the dirt from the shoes that rubs off there was no longer any reason to use crampons, like old women do to keep from slipping. And so there was mass that Sunday, like all the other Sundays; like all the other Sundays, and people from Upper Saint-Martin came; nothing at all happened; even the men from that Saint-Martin stayed a moment to speak in front of the church; and there was Brigitte, because she still had those four little packages in her pocket, she hurried through the village to a sister she had who lived there.

"Goodness," said the sister, "What brings you here?"

"I came to say goodbye."

"I haven't seen you for so long. Stay and have lunch with us."

"I can't."

"Why can't you?"

"I've got to do some housekeeping."

"What?" said her sister, "An old woman like you?"

"It's not for me... it's for Anzévui."

"The old man with the plants?"

"Yes."

"How's he doing?"

"Not very well..." Then she asked, "Where are the children?"

"They haven't come back yet."

"Ah," said Brigitte.

"Oh, here are two of them!"

There were two tall girls who came in just then.

Brigitte took two small packages from her pocket, she said, "I brought you a little souvenir. There's one for each of you."

Everyone was astonished, because Brigitte was poor. Souvenirs? What could that mean?

"Go get your brothers. They must be at the cafe. Tell them their Aunt Brigitte is here..."

This is what the mother said to the oldest of the girls, who went out and came back just after with two boys about twenty years old.

And Brigitte handed each one his small package. They said, "Can we open them?"

It was a five franc piece.

They said, "Oh, thank you!"

She said, "It's a souvenir."

But they were laughing, "What good luck. This afternoon there's a Shooting Club meeting, and we didn't want to go..."

"They've done their military service, the both of them," said their mother, "they're both riflemen."

"We didn't want to go because you have to drink and it's expensive... but now we'll have something to drink with. Thank you very much!"

TWELVE

It has to be said that right up to the end the season was such that it seemed that those who'd believed Anzévui would be proven right. He said, "It's just that the sun is unwell. It doesn't have enough power to dispel the fog."

He said, "It's fading every day a little more, it's growing weaker, it's getting colder, it's getting smaller; but don't tell anyone so as not to scare them all before it's time."

Which is why Brigitte said nothing. And he just kept sitting beneath his plants, coughing. But those who knew shook their heads, "We can't prove him wrong."

Because even in the deepest part of winter, even in these villages where the sun doesn't show itself all day, nothing is usually more beautiful to see than the pureness of the sky and the brightness of the snow. Even here where we don't see the sun for six months, we feel its presence behind the mountains, from where it sends it delegation of colors—pale pink, light yellow, red, with which a tiny brush draws the mountain peaks around us. The snow on the rooftops is like a white sheet just washed with a blue cloth; the snow piles beside the rooftops are like piles of bed linen, folded in four and showing each thick fold; and the thick folds break and fall sometime, with a squashy sound like a ripe fruit. The snow settles on the tops of the fence posts like lambswool caps. The air is both still and animated with a secret movement; it doesn't breathe, it drinks itself. It's more transparent than crystal, as far as the eye can see, so much so that instead of tarnishing things or making them hazy, it makes them clear, it brings them closer like a pair of spectacles. And there's a moment when the sun, still keeping itself hidden, suddenly lights up the mountains that are farther down the valley, an entire half-circled range of peaks in the distance: they're like a pile of wood shavings just touched with a match. These are the broad vistas of the mountains, and while we stand in the shadow they burst into flames from all around; hundreds of peaks aligned in the sky, all shapes, all colors; triangular peaks, square peaks, peaks with several faces, rounded peaks, peaks that are nothing but a raised ridge, peaks open at the base and so standing alone, like columns, like towers, like tree trunks; pointed ones, worn ones, blunt ones, pointed steps; peaks like a pile of ripe wheat, peaks that are transparent like hardened air, peaks like stacked blocks of air; peaks like an ice cube sucked by a child;—while below them the slopes are a juxtaposition of fields of shadow and light, broken a bit lower down by the stipple of the forests. Everything stretching out into the vast space, everything visible to the farthest sky: even the light mist, like the vapor from a small train, or the one raised by a skier along a ridge. And once night falls and all the lights are out—as many sparkles as there were on the white ground, now there are as many twinkling lights in the black sky.

That winter the snow remained gray, the sky low, everything was sad; even during these last days, it was said that the little light there was grew ever weaker, particularly the Sunday afternoon when Julien Revaz arrived.

"What's going on?" he asked. "My father called for me."

"It's all nonsense," said Follonier. "But okay, all the better for you. Gives you some vacation."

Everyone asked Revaz, "How's the weather down there?"

This was later on in the evening at Pralong's; despite how the days were lengthening, they still had to light the lamps around four o'clock. And the men made their way from their homes to Pralong's, the worried men and the unworried men, their hands in their pockets. They were still wearing their animal-skin hats. They were still wearing their winter clothing, meaning those clothes they had been wearing in December beneath their coats, thick woolen sweaters with long sleeves. Because there was still ice; it would ice up not only at night, but all throughout the day, too.

They had lit their pipes, their cigars.

News of the war hadn't improved.

The wireless had spoken to them around seven o'clock. That was followed by an accordion concert. Just after that, Julien Revaz came in.

He called to Sidonie, "Come on, Sidonie, how about you make them quieter?"

She can stop the music for you just by pressing a button; and, even if they still couldn't see each other through the smoke, at least they could now hear each other; and this is what they were saying:

"Hey, Julien, where are you? Come sit down here. How is it going down there?"

"Not bad."

"And the weather?"

"What about it? It's lovely, it's bad, as expected for the season. One day we've got sun, the next the sky is grumbling."

"That isn't like here."

"So you say," said Julien.

"Yes, it's strange. We've never used so much electricity as we have this winter. And your father?"

"What can I say? He told me to come home. I asked for the time off. I had to tell them down there that he was sick... and you know," he said, "it's even true, he looks poorly, my mother too... so, do you believe it?"

"It's all nonsense!" said Follonier. "Why don't you tell us what you're doing down on the lake."

"Like usual; move the earth back up the hill and prune the vines…"

"You know we haven't been able to do anything up here…"

"We carry the manure. There's been days when it already feels like spring; everyone rejoices and we take off our vests, some even take off their shirts, and then it rains the next day; none of this changes the fact that we're already moving forward and that it already feels really warm when you turn the corner around a wall and the lake comes toward you with its sun."

"It's because they have two of them," Follonier said, "and we don't have any."

He begins to laugh.

"It isn't fair! They have too many, and the rest of us not enough… how do you expect the rest of us to work the land? We have to scratch at the snow like chickens. How do you expect us to carry the manure? The piles would slide on the snow and go to the neighbor's, and the neighbor to his neighbor. Would that work? What do you think, Arlettaz?"

Because Arlettaz was there as usual and Arlettaz was seated in a corner with five or six empty liters; and Arlettaz said, "Thief!" and that was all.

So Follonier laughed again; he said to Julien Revaz, "You see how the rest of us are, not so polite. It's because the rest of us live up here too high and too much in the shadow, because there are too many mountains and they're too close to us; it makes us look sickly, we're like potatoes that have stayed too long in the cellar; it makes us melancholy: not me, but look around… you too, Julien, I see it, I can tell you're not coming from here."

"There are already flowers down there," he said, "there are already birds singing: and then to see that nothing is moving yet up here, and there are some who say that nothing is ever going to move again."

"Ah! Here you go, cheers, Julien! Just a few more days of being patient and then you'll see, everything will be fine. Hey, Arlettaz..."

"Thief!" said Arlettaz.

"Is that all you have to say to us?"

"Thief!"

But we saw that Arlettaz couldn't even stay seated anymore. First a man isn't able to hold himself upright: it didn't matter how deeply he was sunk into his bench and how firmly he was resting on his two elbows: we saw him start sliding to the side, his two eyes were closing, his eyes opened again. What would we have to do about it, huh? Hey, Arlettaz!

He tried to turn his head toward the sound; his head would no longer obey.

So that's how we are that Sunday evening, at 1400 meters, in such dark weather, about fifteen of us sitting together at Pralong's, where the electric lamps only barely managed to brighten the smoke; it looked like egg yolks dripping. Everyone was now looking at Arlettaz. Suddenly, one of his arms slipped from where it was resting on the table, and his head came down onto the brown painted wooden tabletop.

"Hey!"

He doesn't even try to get back up; his hat has fallen to the ground. His beard dips into the spilt wine—because he'd knocked over his glass; his arm is hanging along the length of his body like a broken tree branch. We came over to him, we brought him upright, we resettled him onto his two elbows, we spoke to him but he didn't seem to hear us.

"Hey, Sidonie," said Follonier. "How much does he owe you?"

"There were three liters this morning, four this afternoon and then this evening…"

She counts the liters on the table.

"Five and four and three, twelve…"

"Twelve at 1.50, 18 francs. Well, we'll pay you. And the rest of you, give me a hand."

He rustles in the pocket of Arlettaz's trousers. He said, "My poor Arlettaz, I'm stealing from you again, but I've got to do it."

He withdrew his hand filled with little coins, folded bills, and silver money: "Look at that, you're still rich."

Then, "Everyone can see, right? Five, ten, twelve, fourteen," as he lined the francs and other coins up along the table, "Seventeen francs and fifty cents, eighteen francs; that's the total. And everyone can see I'm putting the rest back from where I took it; if he ever accuses me again, you'll be my witnesses."

He was laughing. The evening was finishing better than it had started. There was something new. They said, "Now we need to bring him home, otherwise he's going to roll along the floor." It took about five or six of them; the others just enjoyed watching them do it. They tapped on Arlettaz's shoulder, they said to him, "Arlettaz, get up, it's time, Pralong's is closing…" It wasn't true. "Are you coming, Arlettaz?" they said. But he was closed up into himself and couldn't even hear. His forehead was resting on his arms and we could only see the bad side of his head sloping back and his ears by his beard. So Follonier took him by the hair, "Come on! Can't you hear?" and he raised his head, but as soon as he let go, the head fell down again.

"Hey," said Lamon, "take him by his feet."

The others had stood up so as not to miss any of the show; they made a circle around Follonier.

"Eh, Revaz, give us a hand too. You take the lower half, I'll take care of the upper half... That's it, pull him to the side. Be careful of the bench. There we go."

He said, "Come on, Arlettaz, be nice. You'll be much better in your bed..."

And then, leaning into Arlettaz's ear, "And you know, if you let us take care of you, your daughter.... Yes, she'll come back."

Suddenly Arlettaz stirred, "Adrienne?"

"You wouldn't want her to see you like this, would you?"

"Where is she?"

"Come along."

"Thief!" said Arlettaz.

He let himself fall down again on the table, but Follonier and the owner had taken him by the shoulders. We opened the door for them. The smoke tried to get out but couldn't because at the same time the fog was trying to get in. There was a fight, a competition between the fog and the smoke, and it made a kind of vault over them as they leaned over. Then, because it was so dark, someone said, "We need a lantern." Someone went to get a lantern. Luckily. Without a lantern we couldn't have even seen the path. Arlettaz was moaning. The lantern went forward, then came those who were carrying Arlettaz by his feet, then those who were carrying him by his shoulders, and Arlettaz hung between them in such a way that his body was dragging along the ground where it was frozen, where it was a mixture of ice and earth, but we couldn't see anything; every once in a while he tried to fight, then he gave up, then he complained; and they said, "We'll be there soon," advancing behind the pale round shape that the lantern cast on the ground. The lights were out in the houses that we couldn't see.

Follonier said, "It's ok?"

They said, "It's ok."

Then there was a moment that it wasn't okay: they placed Arlettaz on the ground. And he stayed there unmoving, like a dead man.

They laughed, the lantern moved on again. They said, "Luckily, the dead aren't heavy."

"Here we are," said Follonier.

The lantern turned to the right, "Go to the front door, see if it's open."

"Give us some light, we don't know where to put our feet anymore."

Because they were hitting up against stones, then they saw that crossing the path were two old stone steps that needed shoveling out from under a crust of earth and ice that made them slippery; so they tried to put Arlettaz on his legs, but didn't succeed.

They had trouble getting through the kitchen door. Usually a dead body is carried away from its home, but they were carrying a dead body into its home.

It was difficult to cross the room because it was filled with so much stuff. They had to use their feet to push aside all manner of objects which were strewn about the floor before they found what had been a bed and that was recognizable as the bed because of its wooden posts, between which there was a pile of dirty rags which were pieces of sheets and the rest of a duvet.

It was about ten o'clock. She was surprised that her husband Augustin had not yet come home. He had left her after supper to go say hello to his parents; which was the house next door. The parents had built a brand new small house for them, only for them, when they'd got married: in this way the old people were among old things, as is fitting; but they, they were young, and so they placed them among new things. She wondered what he was doing. She became quickly bored when she was alone. What was the point of being beautiful, as she was, if there were no hearts to be troubled by it, and no voices for telling it to the world? She had spent a part of the afternoon with Jeanne Emery, she had run into some people going home, she had laughed like she always did and talked; but now there was no one. And when the hand on the alarm clock, which was placed above the oven on a shelf decorated with pink lace paper, had passed the ten, she couldn't stand it anymore, she got up.

She found them, all three of them, seated in the kitchen of the old house. Augustin, his father, and his mother.

They were silent, all three of them.

The old man and the old woman, they were worn down. It was normal that they were not used to speaking, because the blood cools and because they had spoken already so much—one finishes by having nothing else to say. There was a newspaper on the table, but neither Mr. nor Mrs. Antide we're reading it; and this was normal too, of course, because both of them were tired—but Augustin? He was also not speaking, he was also not reading; none of them were speaking, and because she had pushed the door, they turned, all three of them at once turned toward her, three destroyed faces, so much so that Augustin seemed almost as old as his parents.

"What is...?"

They didn't answer. They were like Arlettaz just before.

"Do you know what time it is?"

"Well..." said Mr. Antide.

And Mrs. Antide raised one of her hands which had been placed on top of the other in front of her. She lowered it again as if to say,

"What does it matter? Do we worry about something like time now that we know time is something that will end?"

Isabelle took Augustin by the arm, she said, "Are you coming?"

"And Jean," she said, "Where is he?"

"Oh," said Mrs. Antide, "he went to sleep a long time ago. He doesn't care, he's young. But the rest of us…"

Isabelle didn't seem to hear her. And Augustin let himself be taken away, he followed her; he stretched his hand out in the darkness, asking, "Hey, where are you?" but she had opened the door to their little house, a house that belonged to the two of them, in this way sending the light from the lamp in his direction like a carpet rolled out along the steps of the building. Now all around them on the walls were the family members looking at them; and the artillery sergeant crossed his arms over his chest to show off the stripes on his sleeves. The bed was so high up that you needed a chair to reach it. The bed had a lovely garnet-colored lace coverlet. It was an old fashioned bed with a modern covering; it's because we're young, aren't we?

"Augustin…"

She was lying down beside him, she had turned off the lamp; and there was nothing that could be seen or heard, anywhere, in the vast and silent world. They had been pulled away from it all, transported to another world that belonged to only the two of them. She had closed the doors, all the doors; "I closed everything, Augustin, we're in our house now, just the two of us."

Is she speaking to him with real words or is it from the inside that she's speaking to him? There are many ways to speak to someone.

But a person has to keep trying, has to try one last time: she spoke to him with her foot which went looking for his foot, with her impatient hand, with her body greedy for him; he didn't seem to understand.

He turned to the wall; she called to him, "Augustin! Oh, Augustin…" she said, "are you sleeping? Listen, there's something I wanted to ask you. Will you come with me?"

He didn't even turn over. "Where?"

"Up above. To the peak."

Again he said nothing.

So she said, "Oh, Augustin, are you mute? Or can't you hear me? It's like I'm speaking to you from up on the mountain and you're down below. It's like I'm speaking to you from one side of the valley and you're on the other side. Are we so far away from one another even while we're so close? Augustin, you're not answering. Will you come with me?"

"When?"

She counted. She said, "It must be the thirteenth. Next Wednesday."

He asked, "To do what?"

"Go and say hello to the sun, Augustin. Because it will come back."

But he grumbled something, and then moved away from her, moving even farther toward the wall across the width of the bed.

Thirteen

The next morning Jean was busy in the shed when Isabelle arrived.

He was seated on the larger pile of wood into which sits the small anvil used for beating the scythes; he was busy repairing a shovel, which meant that he had to raise his head, getting the sunlight in his face, even if it was a weak sunlight.

She said, "I came quickly because Augustin went to the village. Luckily, you're here."

He rested the shovel across his knees, "How are you?"

"And you?"

"I'm fine, thank you."

He gave her a military salute by bringing his hand to his curly hair; his teeth were bright white against his face which was the color of the wood used to build a chalet.

He was seated, she was standing. She started again, "Did you sleep well?"

"Well, you know me, I always sleep well."

"Well, I didn't sleep," she said. Then she looked through the open door toward the path that led to the village to see if Augustin was already coming back, but there was no one; however, she would see him coming from far.

"You've got to take your horn, Jean, the horn from when you were watching the goats, and then you'll blow it."

"Why do that?"

"Listen," she said. "I haven't explained it to you yet; its next Wednesday. You know what they're all saying. And well, let's go—do you want to? Just when they're saying that the sun will never come back, we'll go up into the mountain to help it come out. Because it'll come out, you know."

"And Augustin?"

"He doesn't want to come. And you?"

"Sure, I'll come."

"So you go quickly and tell Métrailler because he knows the paths better than we do. Ask Métrailler to take his rifle. I'll tell Jeanne Emery to come, they'll be five or six of us, and we won't tell anything to anyone, we'll leave early in the morning. And you, you'll blow your horn, like when you were watching the goats..."

She kept looking from time to time toward the path; he was laughing, seated on his wood pile; there they are, the two of them speaking, with happy faces, while she played with the pointed ends of her shawl against her chest.

"You were little, I remember, and I was not much bigger than you. Do you remember? When you would go with your goats early in the morning; we were watching from behind the windows. All us girls were watching in our bare feet and our nightdresses; and there was the big white one which always went off ahead, there was the little black one that never wanted to keep up, and Mrs. Emonet who was always late; so you would get angry and you would blow as hard as you could into your horn."

"I remember; it's not so long ago."

"Well, you'll do it again. Rub it with some white powder so it'll be really shiny when the sun comes back."

It's a copper instrument with a black horn mouthpiece; he was laughing.

"A good idea," said Jean, "it'll give us a walk."

"And it'll mark the difference," he said. "Because there are those who live in their rooms and there are those who live outside. We're the ones who live outside."

"I'll get Jeanne Emery to agree. We can meet up at her house. It's just that we'll have to keep it a secret from the others, those who'd like to. You, Métrailler, Tissières, Jeanne Emery, me, and we'll see… Métrailler with his rifle, you with your horn. And we'll make the sun come out from wherever it is, even if it doesn't want to."

"Well, I think it'll want to."

"Because, remember, here in the village it hardly ever shows itself until around ten o'clock; we'll see it before eight o'clock and we'll announce it to them."

"Agreed."

Jean stood up. "Only, Isabelle, since we understand each other so well, can you give me something?"

She said, "What?"

"Oh," he said, "Would you? On my forehead?"

She took him by his two ears. And quickly threw a glance once more toward the path; and then there where it's soft, narrow, there where the bone is just beneath the skin so that the skin is stretched tight; below the spot where the line of hair is thick, like the edge of a wheat field with its stalks rustled by the wind.

"Oh, sure," she said, "and it's just, well, because he doesn't want to."

And it was another gray day, then it was a second gray day. This was near ten o'clock at night. The houses were cut off from the world as the lights went out in the windows, making them a part of the night in the night. The houses gave up their existence, one after another. In the midst of all this death, there was only a faint glimmer that indicated the village square, marking that it was still alive; this was Brigitte's lamp which continued to shine, but hardly; and isn't she going to put it out and what would be left of us if it went out?

Denis Revaz had gone to bed, but had not been able to sleep.

It was maybe eleven o'clock when he said, "Is someone calling me or am I dreaming?"

But someone called him again; so he nudged his wife with his elbow. "Say, Euphrosine, did you hear that?"

Their two boys must have been sleeping for a long time; but he saw that she must have stayed awake, even if she wasn't moving at his side; both of them there not saying anything, the two of them likely thinking of the same things; because she answered him quietly, "What is it?"

"Denis!"

He could no longer doubt that someone was calling him; the voice came from the front of the house; it was both weak and urgent, it was nothing but a whisper and at the same time it was a yell; and he sat up on the bed. He said to his wife, "You stay here!" then he got out of bed without turning the lamp on, put on his trousers, his vest, not making any noise, because of the boys; and all this time someone continued to call him quietly:

"Hey, Denis! Hey! Can you hear me, Denis?"

Then it was silent, then the voice started again, and now he felt he recognized it...

And it was exactly who he was thinking, because he opened the door and saw Brigitte.

"Denis, you've got to come quickly, hurry! Oh, my god!"

He said, "What?"

"Come quickly, his fire's gone out."

"Whose fire?"

Brigitte said, "Anzévui…"

"And so?"

"Well," she said, "he wouldn't have let it go out if… I know him, I do. At nine o'clock there was still movement behind the windows. And I fell asleep. But I woke with a start a bit after, like someone was telling me something had happened; and nothing was moving anymore… Denis, you've got to come."

"For sure I will, but there needs to be two or three of us."

"Call your boys."

He shook his head. "No, not them. But you? Can't you go and get someone else while I get ready?"

She came back with Follonier and Métrailler; this meant they were four. Anzévui's house couldn't be seen from Revaz's house. You had to go to the turn in the path to see it; and that night they couldn't see it. The glimmer of light that marked its place was gone—a little like when the track guard lowers his faded flag. The snow was colorless, it made only a vague glimmer in the depths of the night like a shadow behind a hanging curtain. It was the last night. They came, there were four of them, they finally arrived at Anzévui's door. They went in, and until then they had been in the darkness, but they found themselves again within another great darkness.

"Damn!" said Métrailler, "do I have some matches?"

"I've got some," said Follonier.

They were standing on the doorstep. Follonier struck a match, then held his arm out toward the inside of the room. Only the little blue flame didn't give any light and the brighter flame that came after was still not enough.

"Oh," said Brigitte, "we'll have to go find a candle. There should be one on the mantelpiece, because he lit his room with his fire and only with his fire."

"I'll go," said Follonier.

He struck another match, then stopped.

The silence that filled the room was like something that stopped you from moving forward. Brigitte ended up joining Follonier. The match went out; they bumped against the table, then saw the table, and Brigitte said quietly, "It's there." She held Follonier by the flap of his jacket. And now that the candle was lit, they both went to see.

"What did I tell you?"

Raising the candle, Follonier turned toward the two others who had stayed at the edge of the door and who were coming forward. Brigitte was there, her hands held together, turned towards the arm chair that could now be seen.

She gestured three times in a row.

And in the arm chair was old Anzévui, because he was dead like someone who has fallen asleep, like the lamp that goes out because it's out of oil, like the fountain that stops running because it's out of water, like the silence of the clock when it stops ticking. Only his hands were open; the book had slipped off his knees; his head had tipped to the side; we couldn't see his face anymore, but only his hair and his beard which made a white spot like the kind there are in the high mountains when winter lasts all summer.

"Now what?"

This was Follonier. He couldn't stay long without speaking.

"Now what? He was old, he lived his life, what else is there? He didn't need anything from anyone. We better get to it," said Follonier, "while he's warm."

He placed the candle on the table.

"It isn't only him, it's us," said Brigitte. "The rest of us... oh, go slowly," she said, seeing Follonier and Métrailler moving toward the body and, preparing themselves to carry it; and Denis Revaz hadn't moved from his spot, but we could see his jaw trembling. "Go slowly, please. And where do you want to put him?"

"He has a bed?" asked Follonier.

"Oh," she said, "it isn't made. He didn't sleep there anymore, he had too much trouble breathing. Wait while I clean things up."

So she went to work, and she said, "Give me light," as she moved toward the corner of the room where there was, indeed, an old pine bed made of a simple wooden frame with a straw mattress and some covers. There was no pillowcase over the pillow, no sheets on the mattress. But she smoothed the mattress as best she could with her hand, then she put the pillow where it needed to go; and so they carried Anzévui, meaning Cyprien and Follonier.

"He isn't heavier than Arlettaz," said Follonier, "and he's better about letting us help him; he isn't any better housed than Arlettaz..."

While they laid Anzévui down on the mattress, and Brigitte placed his hands together, and they closed his mouth by tying a handkerchief around his head; then Brigitte said, "I need to go get some holy water and my rosary," and so Revaz said, "I'll go with you."

He didn't come back.

Then Brigitte placed around the dead man the usual things needed when someone leaves us forever; she lit candles, placed a clean tablecloth on the corner of the table: she sat down next to the bed.

She nodded, "It's just what he told me, because he said, 'I'll go when it goes.'"

"Bah!"

"It's a sign that he had clear vision, it's a sign that he wasn't wrong."

"He mixed things up," said Follonier. "He took himself for the sun."

"Oh, be quiet!" said Brigitte.

Just then Métrailler got up from his chair.

"You're leaving us?" asked Follonier.

"Yes, I have to go. I'll send someone else to you."

"I'll stay here a moment longer."

"I'll stay here the whole time," said Brigitte. "Only, Cyprien, check if my lamp is still burning when you pass by."

That same night, she—Isabelle—woke at five o'clock. Because even in cloudy weather, the daylight comes early in April. She moved one knee, she moved the other. She moved them just enough so that Augustin finally says, "What are you doing?" but without really waking up. "I don't know, I'm thirsty, I'm going to drink a glass of water in the kitchen." She slipped from the bed. She didn't light the lamp. Her feet were light and careful. She went out of the house. She was then in the snow and in the night, but the path was not long, and soon she saw the windows of Jeanne Emery's room glimmering because they were already lit. And beneath Jeanne Emery's windows, she only had to say, "Jeanne, it's me."

"What time is it? They're going to come," said Isabelle.

"Oh," said Jeanne, "We have time."

"Are you ready?"

"I'm ready."

"And my outfit?"

"Here it is."

Isabelle's skirt and bodice were laid out beside each other across the bed. "Only," Jeanne Emery said, "I'm afraid you won't be warm enough, because it's light."

"No," said Isabelle. "I have my shawl."

Then she stood before the mirror, then Jeanne brought forward her electric lightbulb that she had hung on a nail.

"It's just that I was a little short on fabric," said Jeanne.

"It's fine, I have my necklaces."

She laughed and raised her arms before the mirror. Her laughter was like water running, her teeth like little white stones that can be seen moving beneath the water.

"It's tight!"

"Wait," said Jeanne Emery.

Jeanne Emery pulled with both hands on the bodice, "It isn't settled right, and because you're so curvy." Then she said, "We're going to see you in the front down to the base of your throat!"

"It doesn't matter, it's the spring. Where did you put my necklace? And where did you put my earrings?"

The necklace was like a red slash upon her brown neck, the earrings were like two drops of blood that had beaded upon her ears.

Then, tilting the mirror, she looked at herself from her feet to the top of her head; she had little feet in her big hobnailed shoes.

She looked at herself again; her calves were rounded beneath her heavy wool stockings, her waist slender, her neck curved.

"Say, Jeanne, do you think it'll do?"

And Jeanne said, "I think it'll do."

So Isabelle took her shawl and tied it around her chest; and knotted beneath her chin a black kerchief covered in bouquets of all colors.

"Here we go!"

At the same time they heard Jean's voice beneath the windows, "Are you there?"

Isabelle said to him, "Do you have your horn?"

He pulled it out from beneath his jacket.

Then Métrailler and Tissières appeared; Isabelle said to Métrailler, "And you, did you take your rifle?"

But we'd already seen the barrel sticking up over his shoulder.

"And cartridges, Métrailler?"

He rustled in his pocket; he had a handful; they were buck shot cartridges like the ones used for hunting chamois.

"I have them, see, and more than enough. Because how many times should I fire?"

"Thirteen times in a row."

"Why thirteen?"

"Because today is the thirteenth."

They were surprised then because it wasn't just Lucien Revaz, the younger brother, who showed up but also Julien whom they were not expecting.

"You're coming?"

"Hey, you're coming too?"

"Yes," said Julien, "because I'm also eager to see it, I'm missing it."

And then Métrailler said, "You all know that Anzévui is dead."

"Well then, that's it, it's over!" said Isabelle. "Everything begins or begins again. You go in front, Métrailler, you're the one who will show us the path, and then Jean you go after."

She had opened the door and Métrailler said, "Yes, only there are some who believe it's the end for everybody, when Anzévui is dead."

But Isabelle let her laughter be heard, and it was again like the song of the blackbird.

They were quiet at first because they had to go along a part of the street that crossed the village. They walked two by two, Métrailler at the front; Jean was next to Isabelle and she took his hand. To the east, at the end of the village, Brigitte's lamp shone softly behind her window panes. And then they saw that another window was shining that night, and much more than usual, with a stronger light, less flickering, steady; it was the candles which burned upon the corner of the table in Anzévui's kitchen.

And so they passed in silence next to Anzévui's house; they began to climb the mountain. The snow was frozen because it hadn't stopped freezing in the night. But the daylight had begun to melt it from above, in such a way that its thickness had already decreased. Métrailler walked at the front, and the path he cleared was taken up by Tissières, then by the others, and widened; while below them the village continued to sleep beneath its many little roofs that could barely be seen, their edges barely outlined by a blue line. No change was yet visible around them, neither at their feet; they had to get themselves much higher before the snow finally took on a kind of color. Was it really a color, though? We see something pale come to life little by little above us, without an outline or edges, but a vague clearness was becoming apparent all the same: the daylight is born below, and they were carried by it into the air still filled with night. Should you blow your horn, Jean? No, not yet! Because above them was a ridge not far away, but that they had to reach, because from there we can see both slopes, there we stand where two mountain sides meet each other; we can lean to one side, we can lean to the other, and below us lies an entire country to one side, and then another entire country to the other.

And so aren't you going to blow your horn?

There were seven of them, they arrived upon the ridge. The snow up there had been swept by the winds. It's up here that the winds are stopped by nothing, that they blow from the north or from the south. The group of them found themselves face to face with this wall of stone blocks placed one on top of the other and which suddenly have a color and a shape; they have become gray and we see that they are gray; they're not only gray, but veined, and we see their veins, and they're spotted and we see their spots. In the emptiness which they leave between them a little bit of snow had remained, we saw the snow; in other places we saw the earth and there was upon it a little bit of yellowed grass. Yellow, white, gray, and brown.

And so Isabelle held out her arm, "Look down there; what did I say?"

They stopped. We saw her now, saw her; and she too, she saw them. We saw the color of their faces, we saw the color of the clothing: Métrailler's gaiters, Tissières leggings, Julien Revaz's mustache; and her, her tanned cheeks which were in their element like a peach as it ripens.

"It's going to be sunny. Blow in your horn, Jean, so that they hear us in the village. Blow like you did in the army. Tell them, "Rise up, elders, the moment has come."

Jean blew in his horn.

So we saw the village re-born to itself little by little. From up above, they saw it revived by the light, having lowered their heads just as Jean brought the mouth of his instrument to his face. The air was cleaned between them and him, the air became completely transparent; and down below the roofs were perfectly visible, lined up one against the other, making light blue squares which leaned in different directions. Jean's horn drew them: and above the blue of the roofs, another lighter blue began to move about like waves that the wind blows gently along the lake in fine weather. They came, the people down below came to light their kitchen fires. The women were in front of their ovens or leaning over the hearths; they said, "What's that sound?"

They raise their heads, they say, "What's that sound? But that's the shepherds horn for the goats"; then, turning towards the window, "Look at that! The weather is going to be fine today."

"Oh, little one, what's wrong?"

Justine Emonet picked up her child and held him against her, lifting him in the air; she pressed her head against his head and, cheek to cheek, she spoke to him; but the child just held his toothless mouth open in his bright red face and his eyes were hiding behind the folds of skin that his crying created, suddenly he lost his breath, and there was a long silence, from which came only a kind of ragged breathing.

"Oh, what is it, little one? Are you in pain? Is this the end?"

But then the daylight came in through the window; she went over to it, she stood within it; then she turned the child into the full light. "I can't even see his eyes he's crying so much, but he is red, a lovely red. He wouldn't be so red if he wasn't healthy. Maybe it's only that he's hungry?"

She sat near the window, she opened her bodice. And suddenly the crying stopped. She took her breast in her hand, she leaned forward; the little down-covered head turned to the side. And he made a little sound because of the little something that goes from me to him, because of what was shared.

And so she stopped moving; she only raised her eyes, not even her head; and a smile was upon her tilted face like a second light, even if through the little windows she was only watching the snow turning pink, as if the carnations in her garden had all bloomed at the very same time.

Up on the mountain, Jean Antide was blowing his horn; and Mrs. Revaz called to her husband, "Denis! Denis! Come and see... you were wrong... the weather is turning fine... we're certainly going to see the sun today"; And up on the mountain, Jean Antide said, "There we go," and he put his horn back inside his jacket, because Isabelle said to him, "That's enough for now."

Then to Métrailler, "We have to walk the ridge to Sézymes. Can we? Tell us, Métrailler."

"Of course we can, because the weather is so fine."

They walked along the stone backbone which was then an earthen backbone; they walked, sometimes on the rock upon which their shoe nails squeaked like teeth against a bone, sometimes on a thickness of grass which was like a felt carpet beneath their feet. After, they arrived into a clearing where several larches were growing and which looked like bits of gray smoke pushed to the side by the wind; but just through this smoke, what did we see to our left?

"Jean, blow your horn!"

He blew his horn and Métrailler held out his hand to Isabelle; when the going was difficult, Métrailler, who was taller than she was, pulled her forward, Jean pushed her from behind.

"Hey, Jean, look, blow again."

The horn began to shine.

And she said, "I'm too warm."

They stopped again on a peak; they began to see the earth spread all around them; the sky above them began to clear. She said, "I'm too warm." She took her kerchief off her head.

We saw her neck—brown and pink—we saw her earrings, we saw her hair upon which a little snow had melted and made droplets, and they were like dew on the tips of the grass, shining in the daylight.

"Oh," she said, "Aren't we going to get there?" And her chest rose beneath her shawl.

"We're almost there," said Métrailler, "There's just a last bit. We'll be up there at just the right time. Hey, you... golden girl..."

"Both of you..." looking at Isabelle, then at Jean, "You golden ones. There's the rest of us, the burned ones, isn't that right Tissières? Well, we're pulling you up. You just have to let yourselves be pulled."

The clouds on the horizon were gathering into bunches like milk does when it curdles; the bunches were gray, they became pink, they stretched out in regular lines and trembled like clouds made by the water in the sand near the ocean. And it began on the left. A first point appeared there, like a candle with its flame. The group of them was still in the shadow, but over there to the east, one after another all the fires were now lit. And not only the ones we dreamed of, not only the ones we invented ourselves, not only those that appear when you close your eyes like before;—but the real ones, true ones, ones we can see, ones we can touch, that pull your glance outside yourself, that rip you from yourself. The mist was rolling into balls which were placed one atop the other like balloons ready to be launched, from some flat meadow on the mountain; and one after the other all these rounds and balloons were let go, leaving behind them a thousand visible points, with their brilliant dresses, kneeling in the morning.

"Blow, Jean: or if you've no more breath..."

He blew again; there was nothing else in front of them but a last hillside that they went up. Then all at once the sky turned golden above the mountains; with the sun's rays it was a great fan opening wide.

Isabelle said to Métrailler, "Get ready!"

"It isn't quite there yet."

So she said, "I'm too warm."

It's just that the air was warmer and warmer, it was also because they'd been exerting themselves.

"You see," said Lucien Revaz to his brother, "it was a good thing you came."

At the same time she took off her shawl, and we saw her red necklace at the base of her naked throat.

"Oh," said Jeanne Emery, "now you can really see that your bodice is too short!"

"Oh, well," and then to Jean she said, "Do you think so, too?" She laughed and moved her lovely shoulders beneath the thin cloth.

"It's coming?"

"Not quite yet."

"Too bad," she said, "It's too bad we can't go down now to our summer chalet. It's just below us."

"I know," said Métrailler, "but there's too much snow and it's going to start to melt."

"Too bad! We could dance in the chalet. Jean, do you have your harmonica? Well, keep it in your pocket, and we'll go there when it's time to cut the hay together; it'll be soon now," she said. "Time is passing quickly... what do you say, Jean?"

Then, "Métrailler, are you ready?"

She was in front of all of us, she turned her back to us: we could see her braids hang down over the nape of her neck like a bunch of dark red grapes.

And just then the soft hair on her cheeks blazed with light, at the same time as the outline of her neck and the contour of her shoulders were drawn with a line of fire.

Métrailler raised his rifle into the air.

One, two, three, four... that's what they counted in the village. They said, "Where are they shooting from?" They counted to thirteen.

And neither Brigitte nor another old woman who were sitting watch over Anzévui had moved; but then they heard a fly who had woken and began to buzz somewhere in the room.

"So," said the old woman, "How about that? It seems he was wrong..."

Brigitte didn't answer, but she got up; she went to get a sheet, she drew it across the dead man's face.

Ω

First would be Ulysse, because he's the first to rise. But he doesn't like getting out of his bed; he'd go right back to sleep. Just enough time for him to think it can't be time to get up because there's no daylight yet. And he would have let his head fall back against his arm with its big hand sticking out.

At the same time, Madame Favre—who is sitting watch over her child, who's had a fever for three whole days, so she hasn't slept for all that time—would begin to feel surprised at the length of this night. She would think it strange how slow the hours pass when one doesn't sleep. And taking up the teacup with her herbal tea, she would lean over the small head in the scoop of the pillow.

Then maybe Larpin would come along. He doesn't sleep much because he's old. He has the anxiety of the elderly, which make them unable to stay still for long; and so once he's awake, he has to get up.

Which is what he's just done, and his big watch with its round crystal hangs from the wall. He has gone to check the time on his watch. He shook his head. He took his watch down from the nail where it hung and he put it to his ear. He listened a long while. But the little sound of the watch's beating heart could still be heard beneath the metal case; the small ticks kept coming, regular. He didn't know what to think. He thought his watch must be fast, but it's never been before.

We see him cross the room, and then he opens the door. Once

he's in the kitchen, there is another door. He opens this second door and walks the length of the hallway.

He has kept a hold of his watch and the steel chain hangs down between his fingers.

He goes to the front door; silently, he pulls the latch.

And there, as he opens the door, a night like he's never seen before presses down upon him. He backs up a bit. He still hasn't understood. Again, he presses his watch to his ear and he shakes his head, all the while looking outside.

Above the collective mass of the gardens and the fields, he sees a huge black sky filled with white stars. These stars appear to be painted across the sky with a brush. They give no light, these stars.

We can see nothing but the blackness and the white of these stars. There is no wind, and yet it's very cold. Everything seems to be tightened into itself, hardened. The air itself is brittle and we think of glass. Larpin wonders what is going on.

The village is still sleeping and this reassures him for a moment. Maybe he's actually woken up at the wrong time, or he's having a bad dream. But all of a sudden his muscles tighten below his Adam's apple, pushing it upward; he breathes with difficulty. The need to shut his door comes upon him, he closes it, and he stands behind the door, not knowing what to do, waiting.

Five o'clock rings, and we can see it isn't yet light out.

Yet this is May. The five bells ring out, and it seems like the sound they make has doubled, even tripled in strength. They ring and echo and echo for a long time, as if they are hitting sheets of metal. It's impossible for us not to hear them. And Larpin moves his head forward. He rests his forehead against the door panel, he listens, the clock rings again, each new ring growing quiet in its turn, then a door opens, then a second door, then a long call rises up in the dark.

He recognizes the voice of a neighbor, and she's calling her husband, "Julien! Julien!" We hear Julien answer her, "This is the devil's work." A third voice comes in from the opposite side, "What's going on?" And now, from all around, the voices cross and question each other.

He dares now, he opens his door again. Standing on the threshold, he looks all around him, but none of us can see anything but the red dots of the lanterns moving about. They are nothing but dots, they give no light. Above are the white dots of the stars, below the red dots of the lanterns.

He coughs, he feels the cold creep up his legs; yet he remains where he's standing because he needs to feel the life all around him. From where he's standing, he, too, shouts out at random into the dark night, "What's going on?"

A voice comes back to him, but it's impossible to say from where.

He speaks again but his voice trembles, "There's no way all the clocks jumped forward at the same time."

He recognizes Julien's voice responding to his own, "I'm saying this is the devil's work."

The air smells musty, like a cellar. No need to see the people to know that no one is moving. We can feel that all around the square, on each threshold, the people have stopped, and they are calling to each other through the thickness of the shadow, and they speak to one another through the shadow, but no one dares move forward.

Suddenly, the sound of steps can be heard, the sound of someone coming quickly, shuffling in heavy, untied shoes. Then a great cry; and now everyone knows it is Crazy Rose.

She runs in front of you all, no one sees anything, but her voice and her cry pass just alongside all of you, sending a shiver down each of your spines.

Hers is the shriek of a wild animal. The shriek an owl makes from up high in the barn when it opens its beak, and over the thick down of its feathers, lets loose an anguished, lamenting, strangled wail. And it goes down, and then it rolls low, and then becomes piercing once again. And this was how Rose's shriek sounded as she ran past in the big shoes she didn't have time to tie, the heels slapping on the pavement.

Oh, God! Is it possible? Because this shriek is the shriek of death. Larpin stands in his doorway, and he says, (in a tiny, woman's voice), "My God, my God, is it possible?"

All the women begin to cry.

*

I think of you that morning. Because you're lazy, it will already be seven or eight o'clock when you wake up in your snug room, with the shutters and curtains closed. And once you've left your warm bed, your first movement will be to stretch and open your arms. Then you will yawn.

You love long nights and deep slumber when all is forgotten. You will regret leaving that behind. But suddenly the idea of the new dress you laid out on the back of a chair will come to you. You'll be happy at the thought that in just a moment you will try the dress in front of your mirror. It's a white dress, and white suits you well. And you will smile to yourself.

You become sad only when you notice there are no bright bands on the cloth curtains, traced by the sun as it passes. All is dark, and you think that the weather must be bad.

This is a big disappointment for you. First, you'll think only of staying in bed, then you'll tell yourself to go look. One can never be sure.

Just time to slip your naked feet into your little red slippers, just time to wrap yourself up in a big shawl, and you tiptoe, curious now of the darkness, curious also of the coldness you feel, which is an unseasonal cold although sometimes there are late cold snaps.

You pull the rope; the wooden rings slide on the rod and click as they hit one another. You must look for the latch with your hand, how strange. And once the bar is open, even though the daylight has plenty of room to pass through, you have to search with your hand to find the rod for the shutters.

As the night comes to you, so do the cries. What are the women crying about?

But you forget these cries for what comes before your eyes. A black hole, an abyss, like a dark mouth, with a breath that blows on your face. And even you, you don't understand either. No one understands right away, but you retreat sharply to the back of the room. And then you open your mouth a little, trembling, wondering.

You see the ice cube stars, they must be sending this great cold. You need warm clothing but you don't even think of going to get some. You must at least go outside, but you don't have the courage. You can no longer move; and there are only your teeth which start to chatter, a small noise amidst the cries which are now coming from all around.

So, suddenly, you cry out also. And who do you call? You call me, even if you know I won't be able to come. I'm too far away, you know this, but you need someone and so you cry out to me.

You no longer scorn me. You have forgotten your laughter and your mocking from before. You've even forgiven me for them, even if this is something one cannot forgive. You aren't angry at me any-more for the bad things you did to me. You're behaving now. You are nothing but a frightened little girl. You're cold and you want someone to warm you up. You're thinking of your hands, thinking that I would hold them. But what dryness in your throat and on your tongue! What gravel ravaging your voice, what a sound at the end of your words! And the more you cry, the hoarser it gets, the more your words are broken up.

You are nothing but a cry, little one, and just a weak cry at that! Every once in a while you stop. No one answers you. There is noth-ing but the shrieking of the others, but each cry is like yours, each cry flies off for itself, and there is no response for them either, all these cries rising up to who-knows-where – and yours aimed at me, but I cannot hear it.

And then, a moment later, you go out; and then you understand that it's all useless.

You feel that you are alone, alone forever. First comes the shock of solitude, on the threshold of the unknown opening itself up, the unknown of death.

We can no longer doubt that this is death. It blows from above and below at the same time, it hangs from each star. This is death with its open mouth. Death's breath comes into the house, making the curtain folds swing. And this night is the face of death approaching nearer and nearer. So you back away, but the wall stops you.

You tell yourself you are going to die. You breathe in but it's a fu-tile action, and suddenly your voice is like a string breaking, because it has no space to pass.

But you still have your thoughts. You wish again that I were with you. Maybe dying together would be sweeter. Suddenly you love me with the same force you didn't love me with before, with all your solitude and your fear and with this death, too. You had never imagined it before, you had never thought before of this word—forever.

Now you think of this word. It takes you a moment to realize. And then you feel thousands of little pricks at the roots of your hair; at the same time their softness falls away and they stand on end.

Now is when you realize. How will it be? What will there be? First there is a coldness. And then there is night. It will be like this night, but even deeper. And there will not only be this bed to take away, but the wall, the curtains, the room, and also beyond the garden, the houses of the village, the entire village. Not only the entire village but the fields around the village, and the woods around the village, the lake, then the mountain and then the far away countries and their seas, and all that is on this earth. All the way to the blackness of the sky, the whiteness of the stars. All this removed, taken away—And you, too, the center of this world, removed, taken away.

Still, between your eyelids, a last final weak tremor of some kind of color. Still, at the tips of your stiff fingers, a last movement of life. A small effort in the hollow of your chest, but it's already giving way. And around your heart, a kind of hand tightens, while this thing approaches, this thing which is the negation of all things. This forever thing.

This thing that you see for the very first time. You laughed too much, little one, it took up all your time. Along with your clothing, your change of hairstyle and fashion. It's true, you didn't have time. But now you have the time.

And then, suddenly, with a tremendous unconscious effort, your voice has come back to you. Again, you call out, you call out, you call out. You're like the well pulley, a badly greased wheel, like a little frog, or a cricket on a summer evening. You call out, you call out. You call out to me. My revenge is not to hear you, poor little girl flattened against the wall, with this thing approaching, while outside now, the stifled cries, the wailing of the children, the sobbing of the women, the whinnying of the horses, the barking of the dogs, the mooing of the cows, the music of dancing and the drunken songs rise up and join together – because faced with death, there are some who wish to keep living, and, beneath this great shadow that is already covering them, they push their love for life to an insanity for life, preferring to feel it break inside of them rather than have it taken away and feel it slowly slip away.

Ω